Praise for *FINS*

"Kids who enjoy adventure, science and sharks will be hooked by this swashbuckling story."

—*Tampa Bay Times*

"This well-paced, exciting series opener will keep readers on their toes."

—*Kirkus Reviews*

"Give to readers looking for science-based mysteries."

—*Booklist*

"Filled with scoundrels, humor, sharks, intrepid kids, and a surprise ending all wrapped around an environmental theme. Prepare yourself for a fast boatload of fun!"

—*Robert F. Kennedy, Jr.*

"Part detective novel, part field guide, and 100 percent authentic Florida, this fun and suspenseful tale shows Randy Wayne White is an undisputed master of his craft, and this place."

—*John Rasmus, former editor in chief at*
National Geographic Traveler, Men's Journal, *and* Outside

Praise for *STINGERS*

"Something for everyone but especially fans of fast-paced eco-fiction."

—*Kirkus Reviews*

Also by Randy Wayne White

SHARKS INCORPORATED

Fins

Stingers

CROCS

SHARKS INC.

RANDY WAYNE WHITE

ROARING BROOK PRESS
New York

Published by Roaring Brook Press
Roaring Brook Press is a division of Holtzbrinck Publishing Holdings Limited Partnership
120 Broadway, New York, NY 10271 • mackids.com

Library of Congress Cataloging-in-Publication Data
Names: White, Randy Wayne, author.
Title: Crocs / Randy Wayne White.
Description: New York : Roaring Brook Press, 2022. | Series: Sharks Incorporated ;
    book 3 | Audience: Ages 8-12. | Audience: Grades 4-6. |
Summary: After a summer of tagging sharks off the west coast of Florida, Sabina,
    Maribel, and Luke have a new assignment: searching for "survivor trees" that are
    resistant to the disease that is destroying the state's citrus trees; the search takes them
    to the remote mangrove islands of Sanibel Island, where they discover Spanish oranges;
    a grave; an immense saltwater crocodile; a reclusive woman who believes that the ghost
    of a dead king, beheaded by Spanish explorers, is haunting her; and her neighbor who
    is involved in the illegal reptile trade—and in their effort to protect the woman and her
    animals they are soon plunged into a struggle for survival.
Identifiers: LCCN 2021035117 (print) | LCCN 2021035118 (ebook) |
    ISBN 9781250813510 (hardback) | ISBN 9781250813497 (ebook)
Subjects: LCSH: Wildlife conservation—Florida—Sanibel Island—Juvenile fiction. |
    Wild animal trade—Florida—Sanibel Island—Juvenile fiction. | Wildlife rescue—Florida—
    Sanibel Island—Juvenile fiction. | Survival—Juvenile fiction. | Ghost stories. | Sanibel
    Island (Fla.)—Juvenile fiction. | CYAC: Wildlife conservation—Fiction. | Wild animal
    trade—Fiction. | Wildlife rescue—Fiction. | Survival—Fiction. | Ghosts—Fiction. |
    Sanibel Island (Fla.)—Fiction. | LCGFT: Novels.
Classification: LCC PZ7.1.W4466 Cr 2022 (print) | LCC PZ7.1.W4466 (ebook) |
    DDC 813.54 [Fic]—dc23
LC record available at https://lccn.loc.gov/2021035117
LC ebook record available at https://lccn.loc.gov/2021035118

Our books may be purchased in bulk for promotional, educational, or business use. Please
contact your local bookseller or the Macmillan Corporate and Premium Sales Department at
(800) 221-7945 ext. 5442 or by email at MacmillanSpecialMarkets@macmillan.com.

First edition, 2022 • Series design by Cassie Gonzales
Printed in the United States of America by LSC Communications, Harrisonburg, Virginia

10   9   8   7   6   5   4   3   2   1

For Wesley Manning White, saltwater born,
the newest member of Sharks Incorporated

ESCAPE CREEK

Oyster Shoals

Dinkins Bay

DINKINS BAY MARINA

DOC FORD'S LAB

WOODRING'S POINT

CAPT. PONY'S HOUSE

DANGEROUS NEIGHBOR

BONEFIELD KEY

SURVIVOR TREE

LADYFINGER LAKES

BONES GATE

N

W

E

S

DOC FORD COUNTRY

ONE
SHARKS AND SURVIVOR TREES

When the shark jumped into the boat, ten-year-old Sabina Estéban jumped out and hit the water with a splash. Immediately, her flotation vest inflated.

The girl surfaced and grabbed a rope. Her thirteen-year-old sister, Maribel, was in the boat trying to calm the small blacktip shark by covering it with a towel. Marine biologist Dr. Marion Ford—Doc Ford to most—had taught them to do this if a fish got loose on the deck.

On the west coast of Florida, there were hundreds of islands and bays to explore. Boaters had to be prepared when unexpected stuff happened.

"Why'd you jump in the water?" Lucas O. Jones, age

eleven, complained. "Dang it, you probably scared every fish around for miles. You know the rules."

As members of Sharks Incorporated, the three kids had also been taught about boating safety. One of the more important rules? To never, ever get in the water while fishing.

"I was trying to make room for the shark," Sabina sputtered in response.

The girl threw her wet hair back. She was as surprised as the others at what she had just done. One moment, the shark had been at the end of her fishing line. The next moment, the fish had rocketed clear of the surface, whopped her on the chest, and landed at her feet.

Maribel was captain of the small boat—a skiff, it was called—they had borrowed from Dinkins Bay Marina on Sanibel Island. As captain, she was supposed to remain calm no matter what. "Don't worry about it now," she said. "Climb out of the water. We have a lot to do."

Embarrassed, Sabina followed the instruction.

Luke measured the shark. "Sixteen-point-five inches," he said. "This little guy isn't even two feet long." He used the digital scale, reading, "Forty-six ounces—less than four pounds. We've landed sharks a lot bigger than this. No one had to jump in the water before."

Maribel wrote the information on a card. Sabina used a needlelike device to insert a tiny tag into the shark's dorsal fin. The tag and card were stamped with the same code number. Years from now, if the shark was caught again, scientists would know if the fish had grown, and how far it had traveled.

Gently, the kids revived the shark and released it into the water.

Maribel checked the stopwatch around her neck. "Two minutes forty-one seconds," she said. "Not good. We cut that way too close."

Maximum release time was three minutes. Any longer, a shark might not survive. All summer they had tagged small sharks as part of a research program created for kids their age. The trio had become a team—Sharks Incorporated. They had learned to work quickly and professionally. As a team, they had tagged and released a total of 163 sharks. They had also helped bust a gang of shark poachers and earned a $50,000 reward.

This was their slowest release time ever. Sabina knew it was her fault.

"Don't sweat it," Luke said. "That shark's gonna be fine. See how fast it swam off? We all screw up sometimes—but, hey, try to stay in the skiff. Okay?"

This made Sabina feel even worse. One of her secret pleasures was teasing Luke, which he usually tolerated in silence. Why was he being nice to her? The girl fretted about her mistake on the ride back to the marina, where she and Maribel lived with their mother on a houseboat.

The next day, Sabina blamed herself when Doc Ford told them, "You kids won't be tagging sharks for the next few weeks. Hannah has something else in mind. She'll be here in a few minutes."

This had to be some sort of punishment. Halloween was only a week away, and Sabina's birthday was a day later, on November first. Thanksgiving break was in just a few weeks.

Uh-oh, the girl thought.

Luke's aunt, Captain Hannah Smith, was kind and funny, but also strict. She was a famous professional fishing guide. That summer, the woman had tested them on seamanship, first aid, and emergency drills before allowing them to venture out in a boat alone.

She was serious when it came to safety rules.

Doc lived and worked in an old house built on stilts over the water. It was early Saturday afternoon. Sabina, Luke, and Maribel waited for Hannah in Doc's lab.

The room smelled of old wood, chemicals, and salt water.

Aquariums lined the walls. The glass tanks sparkled with swimming fish, seahorses, crabs, and bright corals. Sabina loved how the colorful corals looked like rocks, but were actually alive.

"We like tagging sharks, and I think we're good at it," Maribel said to the biologist. "Did we do something wrong?"

Doc was a large, studious man. He had sharp eyes that didn't miss much. "If you goofed up, your secret's safe with me," he replied, chuckling. "When Hannah gets here, she'll explain what's going on."

The wooden floor creaked as he went out the screen door and left the three kids alone.

Sabina was near tears. She waited through a minute of guilty silence. "This is all my fault," she said. "You both know it. But look . . . I promise I'll never jump out of the boat again, if you don't tell—"

"Hush," the older sister interrupted. "Here she comes."

Captain Hannah, a tall woman, appeared in the doorway, her dark hair tied back in a ponytail. She came into the room carrying a rolled-up nautical chart—a map made for boaters. She also carried a computer bag. On her belt were fishing pliers and a multi-tool that contained a knife and other emergency gadgets.

Maribel had the same tool in a belt holster. Luke preferred just a pocketknife.

"Don't tell me what, Sabina?" Hannah asked with a mischevious smile. "That you jumped out of the boat? I overheard you through the screen door. Was this yesterday? Tell me what happened."

Sabina admitted everything. "Doc said we're not allowed to tag sharks anymore. I figured it was because of me."

"It has nothing to do with you," the fishing guide replied gently. "I'm sure he didn't say you're done tagging sharks. The tagging program is too important. And you kids are great at what you do."

Sabina began to feel a little better.

"What Doc meant is that there's another project you might like," Hannah continued. "Later we'll go over what to do if a really big fish jumps into your boat. That can happen. Every few years, someone's injured or killed, because it's so unexpected."

Nearby was a stainless-steel table. She unrolled the nautical chart. "But first, let's talk about the new project. It's sponsored by the Department of Agriculture."

Luke's ears perked up. Before moving to Florida six months earlier, he had lived on a small farm in Ohio. He had raised Angus cattle, pigs, and chickens, and trained dogs as 4-H club projects.

"Does it have something to do with farming?" he asked.

Hannah replied, "Sure does. In a big way."

The woman explained that a disease called "citrus greening" was killing Florida's citrus trees. Citrus included oranges, grapefruits, limes, lemons, and other fruits.

"And not just in Florida," Hannah said. "It's everywhere, spread by a sort of fly that arrived in the US a few years back. The disease has killed millions of citrus trees. But here's what's interesting."

The kids scooched closer to listen.

"For some reason, there are a few orange trees that don't get sick. No one understands why. Scientists call these rare trees 'survivor trees.'"

The Department of Agriculture needed help, the woman continued. A program had been started for students who were willing to search for these rare survivor trees. Scientists wanted to study them in the hope of finding a cure for citrus greening disease.

"Survivor trees," Maribel repeated softly. "Where would we look?"

"Wild places," Hannah said. "Places along the coast where

most people don't bother to go. Trees that don't have the disease produce big, juicy fruit. If a tree is sick, though, the oranges shrivel and turn green. Soon the roots die. Then the tree dies."

She motioned the kids closer to the chart. It showed Sanibel Island. Squiggly lines mapped the water's depth. This was important to boaters.

"We're here," she said, pointing to Dinkins Bay. The bay was a salty lake surrounded by tough, rubbery trees called mangroves. The water was seldom more than six feet deep.

Her finger moved an inch or so to the north. "See all these little islands? They're only a mile or two from where we are right now. Some of those islands haven't been explored for years. The mangroves are too thick, and there are too many mosquitoes. The islands are so small, they don't even have names."

Maribel was studying the chart. "I thought that area was mostly swamp and nature preserve."

"It is," Hannah replied, "but take a closer look. There are a few islands with higher ground. You might find some very old orange trees growing wild there."

Orange trees weren't native to Florida, the kids learned. So these trees were called "feral oranges."

"People have been planting oranges and other types of citrus here for hundreds of years," the woman continued. "It's possible that some of these old trees are immune to citrus greening because the disease is so new."

The fishing guide looked up from the table. "There's no reward for finding survivor trees. But there are prizes for students who participate. If you kids are interested, there's a lot more to learn. Wild orange trees are different from modern citrus. They have thorns so sharp, they can be dangerous. Wear gloves, and you can start searching today or tomorrow. And then over Thanksgiving vacation, you'd have a lot of time to poke around by boat."

"Survivor trees," Maribel murmured again.

Sabina, a poet at heart, liked the term, too.

Luke didn't much care one way or the other. But he liked the idea of exploring the nearby islands.

Before she put the nautical chart away, Hannah gave the trio a history lesson about how orange trees had first arrived in North America. The kids listened as she talked about European explorers and Florida's Native American settlers.

They also learned that descendants of seeds planted hundreds of years ago have long, dangerous thorns. Wild orange trees were different than modern citrus, and everyone needed to wear gloves.

"Okay," Hannah said finally. "Let's get back to what happened yesterday."

Sabina grimaced with frustration. "I already promised I'd never jump out of the boat again."

"And I believe you," Hannah replied. "But now, instead of a small shark jumping into your boat, picture a hundred-pound fish. Or a big stingray suddenly landing on the deck. Out of nowhere, something that big falls from the sky? What would you do?"

Maribel, as team captain, said, "I've never even thought about that."

"Almost no one does," the woman said. "Remember—things can go wrong fast on a boat. If you're not prepared, you're inviting the worst to happen."

They followed the fishing guide outside to where her fast, fancy fishing skiff was tied to the dock.

"Let's go for a ride," she said. "But first put on your PFDs."

PFD stood for *personal floatation device*. The kids had used their reward money to buy light, inflatable vests that looked more like suspenders. The stylish PFDs inflated automatically if they fell into water, floating them faceup in an emergency. Sabina had been wearing hers the previous day when she'd jumped out of the boat.

On the dock, Hannah continued talking.

"I'm not sure myself how I'd react if a hundred-pound fish crashed down onto my deck," she admitted. "So we'll talk it through. With some practice, maybe we can figure out what is *probably* the best way to handle the situation."

She gave Sabina's shoulder a squeeze before adding, "Who knows? Depending on the circumstances, maybe jumping out of the boat *is* the smart thing to do. I doubt it, but we'll see."

TWO
SAVED BY A HAWK!

On their first trip in search of wild orange trees, Luke would have stepped on a rattlesnake if a hawk hadn't rocketed past his ear.

The bird slammed itself into the weeds. Speckled wings battled a buzzing sound. It was loud, like sizzling grease.

The hawk's head pivoted. Two fiery eyes warned Luke to back away.

He did.

The bird sat upright with the snake in its claws—talons, they were called. The bird vaulted skyward carrying what might have been a coiled water hose.

It was a big rattlesnake.

High above the trees, the snake untangled. It fell and hit the earth with a fleshy *thunk*.

Weeds began to vibrate where the rattlesnake landed—there was that fierce sizzling sound again.

Luke wanted to help the snake, but he knew that wouldn't be smart. There was nothing new about his reaction. He'd grown up on a farm, so he liked animals. They were easier to get along with than people.

Maybe the same was true of snakes. Since moving to Florida, he'd seen videos of rattlers, but he'd never seen one in person.

On the ground was a broken branch. The boy stripped it bare and moved cautiously toward the snake. With the stick, he parted the weeds. Yellow catlike eyes stared back from a coil of glassy scales. The rattler's body was as thick as Luke's arm. It resembled a rope basket decorated with bars of cinnamon and gold.

Beautiful, he thought.

"Glad I didn't step on you," he whispered. "That would've been bad for us both."

A long, rocky knob exited the coil—the rattlesnake's tail. Its rattle was a scalding blur.

"Doesn't look like you're hurt," the boy continued. "If you were, I'd take you to that wildlife rescue place. They've got a nice veterinarian there." He pulled the stick back. "You don't have to worry about me. I won't bother you." He searched the trees. "I wonder where that hawk went."

Months ago, the boy had stopped a cat from killing a large baby bird. An osprey, or "fish hawk," as some called them, the veterinarian had said.

Luke hadn't told anyone that he'd pedaled the clumsy chick to the rescue center on his bicycle. Or that he'd visited the place and helped feed the thing a couple of times.

Now he wondered if it could be the same bird.

From the distance came a wild, high-pitched whistling call. Each note higher and louder: *Peep-peep-pee! SAR . . . SAR-SAR-SARR!*

No sign of the fish hawk, though.

Luke's eyes moved to a stand of tall trees that he and the Estéban sisters had spotted earlier from their boat.

"Let's anchor and take a look," Maribel had said.

Tall trees were a good sign. There might be high ground where wild oranges could grow. So they'd anchored the skiff, then spread out to explore. Mangrove bushes and vines were thick on the tiny island. There were no houses or people.

The sisters had gone one way, Luke the other. He had struggled through fifty yards of jungle when he found a mound of seashells that formed a massive, tree-covered hill.

Shell mounds were a good spot to search, Captain Hannah had told them yesterday at the lab. More than a thousand years ago, Florida's Native settlers had lived atop shell mounds. Centuries later, Spanish explorers had arrived on Florida's west coast. The explorers had killed a lot of the Native people. In the areas they invaded, they had sometimes traded seeds or planted orange trees so they'd have fruit to eat on later trips. Grapefruits, oranges, and limes still grew wild on islands like this.

Such places were rare, Hannah had said. Much of Florida's coast was now covered with houses and asphalt.

Luke was excited to find this hidden shell mound in a bay that was mostly muck and rubbery bushes.

The boy's attention returned to the snake. He intended to leave the animal alone. But then the snake flattened itself. It began to carve its way through the weeds toward the top of the mound.

The sizzling sound stopped.

"Guess I'll follow you," he said in a friendly way.

Luke followed the snake until they were at the top of the

mound. Gumbo-limbo trees with muscular, amber bark grew there.

An animal of some type had dug a hole near the roots, scattering heavy seashells all around. The boy watched the snake slide and disappear into the hole.

"At least I know where you live," he said. "I'll tell Maribel and Sabina to leave you alone."

After a silent moment, he changed his mind. This time he spoke without moving his lips. "Naw . . . I shouldn't mention you to Sabina. First thing that girl will do is call me a pig farmer and make me prove I really saw a rattlesnake. Then she'll try to talk to you. Sabina claims she's a witch. Isn't that nuts?"

It didn't cross the boy's mind that *he* often spoke to animals. And it didn't bother him that, aside from a dog's wagging tail, he'd never received a response.

It was a hot October Sunday afternoon. Mosquitoes swarmed, which was why Luke wore pants, a long-sleeved shirt, and gloves. From a backpack, he opened a second bottle of water and drank it down.

The snake didn't reappear. Luke crept closer to the ground, interested in the seashells.

"Biggest I've ever seen," he muttered.

The shells were the size of bricks, bleached white by centuries of sunlight. The largest shell was unusual. It was decorated with three perfectly round holes. The pointed end had been sharpened like a spear.

Cool. A thousand years ago, maybe a kid his age had used this shell as a tool. The kid might have hiked this same mound while slapping mosquitoes. It was a fun possibility to imagine.

That shell's what some call an artifact, Luke thought. *Probably shouldn't touch it.*

He moved the thing with his shoe into a patch of sunlight.

A design, barely visible, had been carved into the shell. He was trying to make sense of the design when a low, throaty growling noise caused him to spin around.

A motorcycle's growl, it sounded like at first. But why was a motorcycle on an island that had no roads or houses?

The boy cupped his hands to his ears. He heard it again—a low rumble that vibrated through the shells beneath his feet. It sounded more like a lion.

Next he heard Maribel call, "Luke . . . come here. Quick!"

Maribel, despite her age, was usually calm no matter the situation. That was why she'd been named captain of Sharks Incorporated.

Something had scared the girl. It was in her tone.

Luke left the seashell and went down the mound in a hurry, crashing through vines and brush.

THREE
A DRAGON?

Maribel followed the low rumbling noise to a pond ringed by mangrove trees. By then the noise had stopped.

"What do you see?" Sabina demanded. The strange sound had scared her. The younger sister got mad when she was afraid.

Maribel pushed some branches aside. She tilted the visor of her cap and took a long look.

"Alligator," she said. "A big one. I didn't know they could growl like lions. Wait . . . now I'm not so sure it is an alligator. There's something different about the shape of its head." She signaled her sister closer. "What do you think?"

On Sanibel Island, alligators were common in the wildlife preserve. They could be dangerous, so you had to be careful.

But usually, they were quiet, lazy creatures that liked to bake in the sun.

"A gator?" Sabina said. "That's all?"

She was no longer afraid.

The girl poked her head through the branches. The pond was stagnant brown. Spoonbills—pink birds with stilts for legs—hunted for fish and shrimp in the shallows. Floating in the middle of the pond was what appeared to be a twelve-foot-long log. But the log was sharply pointed. It had two heavy knots for eyes, and a tail that was as jagged as a saw.

"Mother of stars," Sabina said in Spanish. "That monster could eat us both in one bite. You're right. It's not like any alligator I've ever seen. It's so big. And its nose is too pointed, and—"

Sabina stopped. The creature threw its mouth open. It made a grunting noise that sounded like *whuff-whuff*. In its bottom jaw were spiked teeth that resembled fangs.

"That's not an alligator," she whispered. "It's . . . it's a giant lizard. No . . . a *dragon*." The girl's eyes widened. "And guess what—the dragon has babies!"

Maribel heard Luke crashing through the brush. The boy's Spanish was improving, but he was still a beginner. "Speak English," she reminded her sister. "I need to get some pictures of this." From her pack she removed the waterproof camera they used when tagging sharks.

Swimming toward the giant lizard were several hatchlings, each about a foot long. They skittered across the pond's surface like snakes and made cute chirping calls. The babies were a yellowish color. The giant lizard was blackish green.

"Hear them?" Maribel was smiling. "They sort of sound like baby birds." She tried to imitate the high-pitched call by gulping a few times with her mouth closed. Then she put the camera to her eye.

Luke appeared. Before he could ask, "What's wrong?" he stumbled over a mangrove root. He grabbed for a limb, missed, and belly flopped into the muck.

"Quiet, pig farmer," Sabina hissed. "You'll scare the dragons. Maribel's taking video before they fly away."

"Before they—huh?" Luke was getting to his feet. "Stop kidding around. There's no such thing as dragons."

"That's what you said about ghosts," Sabina replied. She was referring to their recent trip to the Bahama Islands. Luke hadn't seen a ghost, but Sabina had convinced him that she had. "You were wrong then," the girl chided. "And you're wrong now."

Luke rolled his eyes. He liked the younger sister, but

she was *different*. "That's weird even for you. You're saying a dragon made that rumbling noise? Sounded like a motorcycle to me. Where is it?"

"That's just silly," Sabina countered. "Motorcycles can't fly. Keep your voice down. The dragon has babies."

Maribel was still shooting video of the creature. "Step back and let Luke take a look," she said. "He might see something we don't."

It was possible. Months ago, the boy had had a close call with lightning. A bolt had struck the water near where he was standing. Luke had spent the night in a hospital, then several weeks being tested. The electrical shock had left burn scars that resembled feather-like tattoos on his shoulder and hand.

Doctors claimed that lightning had nothing to do with Luke's excellent eyesight and hearing. He'd been born with those natural gifts, the doctors told him after more tests.

They also said the boy was lucky to be alive.

That much Luke agreed with. Only a fool would stand outside in a thunderstorm. He had never experienced such terrifying pain.

Even so, he was convinced that something had changed in his brain. Since that day, words, numbers, even people and their moods had colors. There was a lot about those colors he didn't understand. But he had come to trust the blue circle that flashed behind his forehead. His "lightning eye," Luke believed it to be.

The bushes around the pond were thick, but instead of stepping back, Sabina pushed more limbs aside so Luke could squeeze in next to her.

"At first I thought it was an alligator," Maribel said. "But its head is different. A giant lizard of some type? Or maybe a crocodile?"

The boy shrugged. "Doubt it. Those live in Australia, I think." He sniffed the air. "Do you smell something musky?"

Maribel shrugged and zoomed the camera lens closer. "See the babies? Aren't they cute?"

Luke cupped his eyes as if holding binoculars. The giant lizard's jaws were open wide. Two of the babies crawled into the animal's mouth as if it were a cave. Five more scrambled onto the giant's back.

Gently, the jaws closed. The creature began to swim away from where the kids were hiding.

"She's protecting her babies," Maribel said. "Maybe she knows we're here. I'll shoot some more video, and then we'll leave her alone. Doc or Hannah will know if it's an alligator or something else."

When Maribel was done, she put the camera away. "Did you find any orange trees?" she asked the boy.

They started backtracking through the rubbery bushes. Sabina didn't want to leave, still insisting the giant lizard was a dragon.

Luke told the sisters about the oddly carved seashell. He left out the part about almost stepping on a rattlesnake. Doc Ford and Hannah might not let them return to this island where, a thousand years ago, kids his age had lived, and used shells as tools.

"I don't care about old orange trees and grapefruits any-way," he added. "You can buy those in stores."

"Not if someone doesn't find a cure for citrus greening disease," Maribel said patiently. She then repeated what Captain Hannah had explained yesterday. Citrus trees that grew wild in Florida were different from modern trees grown by farmers. The limbs might be covered with long, dangerous thorns. And the fruit—the way it looked and tasted—was different, too. Much better for making barbecue sauce for the marina's Halloween picnic next weekend.

Supposedly.

"You can help us prove it," Maribel continued. "Just before we heard that thing growling—whatever it is—we saw what looked like oranges on the ground. But we didn't have time to find the tree. Isn't that right, Sabina?"

"What's it matter what I think?" The younger sister pouted. "This island has to be haunted. I already told you that. The farm boy won't believe me even when he sees the gravestones we found."

Luke stopped. He lifted up a tree branch. The youngest sister pushed past him, her nose in the air.

"You're making that up," he said, then looked at Maribel. "Please tell me she didn't find another graveyard."

Sabina loved cemeteries. She had a gift for finding them in strange places.

"See?" Sabina said. "No one believes what I say. This island has to be magic in some way. Why else would dragons live here?"

FOUR
GRAVESTONES AND A TREE HOUSE

Hidden by briars were three markers that Luke had to admit might be graves. They were round concrete blocks made of sand and shells. At the foot of each marker was a sunken area overgrown with weeds.

"Gravestones," Sabina said. "Told you so."

"They aren't stone," Luke replied. "Those were made in a bucket. Probably by old-time farmers. Not the Native Americans who built this mound. These markers are old, but not a thousand years old."

He had followed the sisters uphill through a tangle of brush. There were no paths, only narrow tunnels made by animals.

"Don't be stubborn," Sabina said. "You can't make a gravestone from a bucket."

"You can if you know how," Luke said.

At a 4-H meeting, club members had learned to make what their instructor called "pioneer concrete." They'd built a hot fire. Next they had mixed wood ashes with water and sand. Gravel was added to the paste. The mix was poured into brick-sized molds. The bricks had hardened into concrete.

The grave markers here were similar.

"You can tell by the shape," the boy continued. "They were mixed in a bucket and dumped while the cement was still soft. Sort of like a new sidewalk where people leave their handprints. How else could they write on them?"

On the markers were faded names scratched by someone using a stick. The names were difficult to read. The smallest marker was decorated with tiny seashells in the shape of a flower.

At the bottom of the smallest marker were dates. Born: 1950. Died: 1962.

"Twelve years old," Sabina whispered. "This person was almost the same age as me when she died. What flower is that? A daisy? See—it must be a girl."

Sabina knelt and squinted at the faded inscription. "Her

27

name was Peri-something. Periwinkle?" The girl turned. "Periwinkle is the name of Sanibel's main street—and some kind of seashell. Is it a type of flower, too?"

"Periwinkles grow wild around the marina," Maribel put in. "We've all seen them. Bright lavender blossoms." She glanced around at the underbrush, which was mostly briars and cactus. "I bet they grow here, too. They're just not in bloom yet."

"Periwinkle. That's a beautiful name," Sabina murmured. She was squeezing the necklace made of blue-and-yellow cowrie-shell beads she always wore. A gift from special women in Cuba—*santeras,* they were called.

These special women always dressed in white clothing and knew a lot about casting spells. When Sabina and Maribel had still lived in Cuba, the women in white had taken Sabina in as one of their own. That was almost two years ago, before the sisters and their mom had come to Florida.

The girl said a silent blessing over the child's grave, sniffed, wiped her eyes, and decided she wanted photos of the markers. Then she insisted they explore around the graves.

Maribel waited a moment, then asked Luke, "Why did your 4-H club learn to make cement?"

"It wasn't the modern stuff that comes in bags," the boy replied. "In the old days, farmers had to make everything by hand. By adding gravel or shells to the paste, you could pour a concrete floor, then build a cabin or barn over it. For a rock fireplace, they'd use the cement as mortar. It's not as hard as real cement. But it works."

Maribel was fascinated. "I wish you talked more about 4-H, Luke. You know about so many unusual things. Sounds like they taught you how to live off the land—like survival training."

She wasn't exactly right. 4-H meetings had had more to do with building forts in a hayloft, or learning how to garden, or scrubbing a horse before the county fair. But he had also learned to cook over a fire and take care of animals, which Luke figured *might* be part of learning how to live off the land.

The boy was embarrassed by the older sister's admiring tone. He hated drawing attention to himself, which was why he wanted to drop the subject.

"Survival skills, sure," he said. "Where's that orange tree you said you found?"

"Not the tree, just oranges," Maribel corrected. "We were still searching when we heard that giant gator-looking thing growl."

They followed Sabina around the cemetery. It was tough going, the area thick with briars and prickly cacti.

"It was smart to wear gloves," Maribel said. "Maybe next time Hannah will let us bring a machete to clear a path."

Pointing, Sabina hollered, "There's more oranges on the ground! And here's the house where Periwinkle used to live. Let's take a look."

The remains of a tin roof lay scattered in the shade. Nearby was a rectangle lined with pioneer concrete. It resembled a tiny swimming pool filled with stagnant water.

"A rain cistern," Luke said. He had already found a rusty hand pump. "They had well water, too, so they probably caught rain for their plants. Irrigation, it's called. That means they had a garden."

Sabina stood quietly and felt a dark weight in the air. The marina where she and Maribel lived was only a mile away, but this hidden spot in the mangroves seemed like a different world. In her mind, she went back in time almost a hundred years. Periwinkle, a child her age, had lived and worked and played here.

Luke drifted off, too. He pictured a cabin, rows of corn, a cooking fire. Then he flashed back a thousand years to when the kids here had made tools out of seashells. They had probably slept in hammocks and carved canoes out of wood.

He'd come to love Florida. There were a lot of hidden places that were very cool, nothing like Disney World in Orlando. The boy hated crowds and noise.

The silence of the island's history cast a spell. It was hot, with no breeze. A cloud of mosquitoes had followed them from the pond. There were buzzing, biting flies. Take a wrong step, and cactus spines might pierce your shoes.

Maribel said what they all were thinking.

"This had to be a terrible place to live. No bug spray or screens or air-conditioning. People had to make everything themselves. Catch fish, grow their own food." She turned to Luke. "I bet you'd know how to survive here. Because of all you learned on the farm."

Luke avoided lying. Usually. Lying required a good memory. But lying seemed easier than trying to explain.

"Yeah. How to survive in the wild, that's what they taught us. Sort of."

The boy motioned to the other side of the clearing. Several oranges were scattered in the weeds. "Fruit grows wild here. And we all know how to catch fish. Food wouldn't be a problem." His attitude brightened. "If we really got hungry, this would be a great place to snorkel around with a speargun."

31

Luke loved snorkeling. Wearing a mask and fins, he had practiced swimming underwater. He could hold his breath for almost two minutes.

The boy kicked at a fallen log. "Plenty of wood for a fire. And I saw a grove of thick bamboo earlier. It would be easy enough to build a hut. Or a cabin. Get it sealed tight—that would keep out the bugs." He shrugged. "I don't think it would be so terrible to live here."

Sabina wore a puzzled look. "Farm boy," she said, "you can't take five steps without falling down. You expect us to believe you can build a cabin?"

Maribel came to his defense. "Of course he can. Let's collect those oranges while he tells us how."

Luke gulped. He followed the sisters and tried to appear confident. It wasn't easy because he didn't know how to build a cabin. True, he had nailed together a chicken coop once, but the chickens had all escaped.

"A tree house would be better," he suggested. "Out here, you wouldn't want to sleep on the ground. Too many bugs and snakes. We could string hammocks."

"How do you know there are snakes?" Sabina challenged.

The boy wasn't ready to talk about the rattler he'd nearly stepped on. "'Cause if I was a snake, this is where I'd live."

"A tree house, huh?" Sabina said. "How would we get up in the tree?"

Luke had never built a tree house, either. But he could picture it in his mind.

"Use a rope ladder. We don't want to pound nails in a tree. That might kill it. Make a platform out of limbs we find on the ground. Lash the platform tight, then build smaller platforms for a roof and walls."

Maribel said, "See? And he'd do it in a way that would protect the trees." Her imagination went to work on the project. They could use vines instead of rope, Maribel said. All made by hand. To keep out the rain, she suggested, cover the roof with leaves.

"People who lived here a thousand years ago might have done the same thing," Luke agreed. "Early farmers, too. There are tons of vines around. Plenty of stuff to make hammocks, or whatever we need."

He hoped that was the end of the subject.

"I want to do it," Sabina said.

Luke cleared his throat. "Do what?"

"Come back here and build a tree house," the girl said.

This was unexpected.

"Why?" the boy asked.

"Because it would be fun. We could camp out for the night. Build a fire, catch fish for dinner, and gather our own food. Why not?" She batted at the cloud of mosquitoes that had found them.

Maribel loved the idea. "When we get back, we'll ask our mom for permission. And once Hannah hears our plan, I'm sure she'll say yes. Doc, too—he's all for us exploring."

Sabina chimed in, "Of course they will. The marina's only a mile or so away. Practically in our backyard. And Thanksgiving vacation is in a few weeks. That would be a perfect time to camp here."

Luke felt nervous. Could he really build a tree house? He looked up. There were oranges on the ground, but none visible in the tangle of limbs overhead.

He knelt and picked up a couple. Hannah had told them that fruit from diseased trees was shriveled and green. These oranges were large, knobby, and healthy. Yet they looked nothing like oranges sold in a store.

Belted to Maribel's waist was the same fancy multi-tool that Captain Hannah carried. He handed an orange to Maribel. She cut it into wedges, and a mist of juice sprayed out.

"Smells like spicy lemonade," Sabina said. When she tasted the orange, though, her lips puckered.

Luke took a bite. It was sour but good. There were hundreds of seeds inside the thick skin. Fun to spit—sort of like darts, the way they shot out of his lips.

"That's gross," Sabina snapped. "Stop it."

"The tree has to be around here someplace," the boy replied, then wandered off.

No luck, though. Not an orange to be seen among the limbs overhead. When he came back, the sisters were even more excited about spending the night in a tree house that the boy wasn't sure he knew how to build.

Sabina asked if Luke could make a sleeping platform big enough for three people. What about hammocks? Was it cheating to use rope instead of vines?

Maribel said, "A hundred years ago, farmers probably had rope. But when the first people were here, thousands of years ago, they had to make everything from plants that grew wild. Luke, did they teach you how to make rope?"

Sabina pressed, "And what about a place to cook? We should dig a firepit so it'll be ready when we come back. Smoke from a fire would help keep these stupid bugs away."

This started a whole new conversation. Aside from catching fish, what else could they have for dinner?

Luke thought, *Crapola. Just what I deserve for stretching the truth.*

"How long before we have to call the lab?" he interrupted, hoping to change the subject.

He knew it hadn't been long, but it was a fair question to ask. When tagging sharks or exploring alone, their team was required to make contact every two hours. Cell phones were undependable, so their boat was equipped with a small VHF marine radio. The signal couldn't travel far, but Doc's stilt house and the marina were just across the bay.

As team captain, Maribel had to keep track of the time. She checked her watch. "We've only been here half an hour. Let's find that orange tree; then I'll radio Doc. He'll know right away if that thing we saw is an alligator or a giant lizard, or something else."

Sabina insisted, "It's a dragon, not an alligator. Why doesn't anyone ever believe me?"

A gust of wind rattled the treetops. A sudden coolness carried the scent of rain.

Maribel held up her hand, signaling the others, *Be quiet.*

She stood and waited. After another gust of wind, she tested the air with her nose. "Smells like a storm's coming," she said. "We've got to get back to the marina right away."

In Florida, thunderstorms could appear fast. The first warnings included a wind change and a drop in temperature.

When a rumble of distant thunder confirmed it was true, Maribel said, "Okay. We've got to move."

The kids grabbed a few wild oranges. They hurried through the tangled brush to where their boat was anchored in the shallows.

Luke noticed that a large bird was following them. It soared high overhead as Maribel steered their boat through a narrow, twisting creek into Dinkins Bay.

He nudged Sabina. "Fish hawk," he said over the noise of the engine.

Sabina looked up and replied, "It's called an osprey, farm boy."

Luke was used to her teasing. To him, Sabina was the irritating little sister he'd never had. "Osprey, yeah," he said. "I saw the same one earlier when we split up to look for oranges."

Sabina had been watching a mountain of thunderous clouds behind them. "How can you tell? Ospreys all look alike. There are thousands of them in Florida."

Luke shrugged.

He still wasn't ready to talk about the rattlesnake. Or the osprey that had saved him.

FIVE

GOOD GRADES AND A STINKY DOG

The kids beat the storm to the marina by thirty minutes. On the walk to Doc Ford's lab, they discussed the chances of being allowed to return to the island and camp for a few nights during Thanksgiving vacation.

"We found oranges," Maribel reasoned. "A survivor tree must be there somewhere. Captain Hannah will want us to go back. If our mom says it's okay, I'm pretty sure Doc and Hannah will say yes."

Luke didn't have an opinion.

Sabina had an opinion about everything.

"You know how adults are," she warned. "We can't give them a reason to say no. All our chores need to be done. Our homework, too." She gave the boy a pointed look. "How bad are your grades this term?"

"Not as bad as usual," Luke said. Usually, he got straight Cs. But there was a chance he might get a B or two.

"That helps," Maribel said. "We'll have a whole week off for Thanksgiving. They shouldn't mind if we ask to camp for just a night or two."

Sabina was the youngest. She was also the slyest when it came to dealing with adults.

"That's where you're wrong," she said. "We'll tell them we want to spend at least six nights. That way, camping for two nights will seem more reasonable. They'll feel like they won the argument and say yes."

Luke was impressed. Being sneaky wasn't something he was good at.

"Maybe she's right," he said to Maribel.

"Of course I'm right," Sabina said. "In fact, let's tell them we want to camp there for the whole week. Doc's easier to talk into stuff than Hannah. He might even say we can stay for three nights—but it has to seem like his idea. Our mom trusts Doc. She'll go along with anything he says."

Luke rolled his eyes. Sometimes the way Sabina's mind worked was spooky.

They were almost to Doc's lab. Maribel was carrying their waterproof camera. "First we have to show him the video I shot. That was a pretty big alligator—or whatever it was."

"A dragon," Sabina insisted. "Dragons aren't dangerous. Everyone knows that."

The boy frowned when she added, "Once Doc hears about the tree house we're gonna build, he'll like the idea. Besides, my birthday is next week. I'll tell them it's the best present I could ever have."

Doc's dog, Pete, greeted them on the path through the mangroves. Pete was a retriever with a block head and cinnamon-colored curly hair. The dog enjoyed swimming in the bay, which explained why his coat was wet and splotched with mud.

"Yuck—get away from me," Sabina hollered as the dog galloped up. "You've been rolling in dead fish."

There was a swirl of wind from the approaching squall. It carried a foul odor. Maribel wrinkled her nose. "Whew. That dog needs a bath. Luke, do something, or we'll all need a bath."

Pete was an unusual dog. The biologist had found him in the Everglades with a snake's head and fangs still buried in the dog's neck. Pete seldom barked or wagged his tail. He could swim underwater like an otter, and he loved to stun fish by jumping off the dock.

Pete was also stubborn. Luke had spent hours with the retriever working on basic commands and hand signals.

The boy slapped his left leg, a nonverbal command: *Heel.* The dog pivoted in midair and landed at the boy's side.

"Good dog—yes, you are," Luke said.

Pete had yellow eyes like a wolf. His head swiveled from Luke to something invisible, high above the trees. The dog was shivering.

"He's afraid for some reason," Maribel said. "Maybe his nose told him there's a giant alligator out there in the mangroves."

A moment later, lightning grumbled from clouds sailing across the bay. Sunlight dimmed. The air had a chill. The wooden walkway to Doc's old house and lab awaited at the end of the path.

"Pete's not afraid of anything," Sabina said. To block the terrible smell, she pinched her nose closed. Her voice sounded like a quacking duck when she added, "Especially if it's something stinky enough to roll in."

"He's nervous, I can tell," Luke said. "Maybe something was chasing him." The boy searched the sky above the trees.

"You guys go ahead. I'll hose Pete off and make him stay on the porch."

Luke was on the lower deck of Doc's old house, washing the dog, when a shadow dashed close to his ear. Pete was startled by the bird that had just dive-bombed them, and dropped to the deck.

Peep-peep-peep! Sar-Sarrr! The osprey that had saved Luke from the rattlesnake circled twice and dived again. This time its talons snatched a tuft of curly hair from the dog's rump.

Pete gave a yip of surprise. Wolfish yellow eyes glared at the osprey. The dog turned to Luke as if to ask, *Is that bird nuts?*

"Hey, knock it off," the boy yelled to the circling osprey. "Pete's a friend of mine. Leave him alone."

Peeep-pee-peep was the response.

Pete stood stiff-legged, no longer scared. Just interested. He often caught seagulls by surprising them from beneath the water. Retrievers had what hunters called "soft mouths." He never hurt the gulls, but he enjoyed the game.

When the osprey dived again, Pete was ready. The dog took a loping stride. He launched himself off the dock and came within inches of snatching the bird from the air before splashing down into the bay.

Peep-peep-peep SAR-SAR-SAR, the osprey taunted while Luke had to hose the dog and dry him again.

From the top of a nearby tree, the bird watched as Luke and Pete went up the steps to Doc's lab. At the door, the retriever stopped, turned, and made a cheerful whining sound.

Yeah. Pete definitely wanted another chance at the playful osprey.

SIX

SALTWATER CROCODILES AND THE RECLUSE

Dr. Ford was sitting at the computer in his lab. Aquarium tanks bubbled. Seahorses clung to bits of grass with their prehensile tails. Colorful fish drifted and darted.

The kids circled around the desk while the biologist reviewed Maribel's video of the gravestones and the strange creature they'd seen. Outside, the first fat drops of rain began to hammer the tin roof of the old house.

"You're right, this isn't an alligator," Doc said. "It's an American crocodile. A Florida saltwater croc, most call it."

Sabina tugged at her braided hair. She was disappointed. "How can you be sure it's not a dragon?"

The man smiled. "You've got a point. I've never seen a

dragon. Either way, I'm proud of you kids. You knew it wasn't an alligator. Most people wouldn't have noticed that the nose is too pointed. Almost like a spear. And the jaws look a lot toothier than an alligator's. Crocs are rare in Florida. You were lucky to see one."

Maribel wondered if it was wise to go back to the island, let alone camp there. "Aren't crocodiles dangerous? I saw a TV show about them grabbing zebras in Africa. Buffalo the size of horses, too, and dragging them underwater."

"Same in Australia," Luke put in. "Saltwater crocs are man-eaters. I saw a movie where a big one knocked some guys out of a boat and ate them both."

Doc had spent a lot of time in Australia and Africa. "That happens more often than people realize," he said. "Crocodiles kill hundreds every year. But in Florida, saltwater crocs tend to be shy. Not nearly as aggressive as alligators. In fact, some experts call American crocs the 'sweethearts' of the crocodilian family."

In his head, Luke sounded out the word—*croc-o-dill-ian*—while Sabina scoffed, "*Sweetheart*? Even in English that's a silly name for a giant lizard with teeth."

"Maybe so, but it's true," Doc said. "In the state's whole history, I've only read about one, maybe two people being attacked by crocs." He added, "They're very territorial, though, when it comes to protecting their babies. Keep that in mind. Florida crocodiles are a lot different from those found in Australia. Or the Nile crocodiles of Africa. They avoid people."

The man paused, muttering, "Let's hope so, anyway." He began to type on the keyboard.

Maribel didn't like the sound of that. "What do you mean, you hope so?"

The biologist explained that several Nile crocodiles had been found in Florida. That was bad, he said. Nile crocs didn't belong in Florida. They grew to twice the size of alligators. Their bite was eight times more powerful than the bite of a great white shark.

Not only did Nile crocodiles attack humans, but they could destroy all sorts of native wildlife.

The Nile crocs weren't invaders, the man added. They had been captured and smuggled into the United States. Florida was a long way from their real home, but an ideal habitat. Now they were reproducing.

"Some people get a kick out of owning dangerous pets," Doc said. "That's probably how Nile crocodiles got here. It's against the law, but that doesn't mean people don't smuggle dangerous reptiles into the country. Not just crocs. Rare turtles—venomous snakes, too. They sell for a lot of money."

On the computer screen appeared a photograph of a giant Nile crocodile. The biologist placed a photo of a Florida crocodile next to it.

"They both look like dragons to me," Sabina said. "I can't tell the difference."

"Me neither," Luke said. "Is there a chance what we saw is a Nile crocodile?" He sounded hopeful. A dangerous croc would be a good excuse not to build a tree house he wasn't sure how to build.

"Truthfully," Doc said, "only a crocodile expert can tell the difference. And I'm no expert. But I know someone who is."

He typed at the keyboard, then hit the Enter button. "There—I just sent him a copy of your video. He's a pal of mine. He usually gets back to me right away."

Luke said to Maribel, "Until we're sure, I don't think we should risk camping out for even a night unless—"

Sabina cringed. She tried to silence the boy with a burning look.

Too late.

The biologist looked up from the computer. "Camping? What do you mean? Camp where?"

Sabina took over. "On the island where we found the oranges. They were lying on the ground, but we didn't find the tree. Know why? Because we were too mature and careful to stick around."

"I'm sure you were," Doc said wryly. "What's that have to do with camping?"

The girl motioned to a window. It was raining harder. "We knew a storm was coming. Maribel felt the wind change. We always follow the safety rules. So now we have to go back and look for that orange tree. It'll take a lot of time."

Doc was amused. "Why do I get the feeling you're trying to soften me up? Camp out by yourselves, you mean?"

"Just for six or seven days," Sabina said. "We get a whole week off school for Thanksgiving. And the island's only a mile from here."

"A whole week, huh?" The biologist chuckled. "You kids out there alone in the heat and the mosquitoes. No TV and cooking your own food. You're sure that's something you want to try?"

Maribel decided it was time to step in. "I think we'd learn a lot about how hard it was for Florida's early settlers to live here. The oranges we found look healthy. That might mean there's a survivor tree out there somewhere. The island is so overgrown, it could take us a while to find it. Here—look for yourself."

She placed the bag of oranges on the table next to the computer.

The man liked the idea after he'd inspected the oranges. Luke was surprised.

"You kids have grit, I'll say that much for you," Doc told the group. He tilted his wire glasses onto his forehead and held an orange to his nose. "Nice . . . smells good. You're right. These oranges look fine. There're what old-timers call 'Spanish oranges.' Nothing like the ones sold in stores. From what I've read, citrus greening disease has killed most of the modern groves. So maybe you really did find a survivor tree."

"Grit?" asked Sabina. After nearly two years in Florida, her English was good. But American slang was still confusing.

In Spanish, Doc replied, "It means you have courage. Determination."

"We have tons of courage," Sabina agreed. "We're smart, too. Even Luke—sometimes."

For Luke's benefit, the biologist spoke in English. "Camp out on an island, huh? Interesting. Sort of like going back in time. Most people have no idea what Florida is really like. They travel in cars with the windows up. They sleep with the AC blasting. You kids would experience something that almost no one else does. I don't know, though—a whole week could be too much."

"Four nights would be okay," Sabina suggested. She flashed Luke and Maribel a smug look when the biologist seemed to nod his approval.

"You have a few weeks before Thanksgiving vacation," Doc reasoned. "Maybe we can find someone to teach you about camping in the mangroves. Hannah and I can help with the basic skills. Fire starting. Where to set up your tent. What to do if there's an emergency. But in Florida there's a lot more to it than that."

Sabina chimed in, "Luke says he learned survival skills at that 4-H club. He's going to build a tree house. Right, farm boy?"

Doc gave the boy a veiled look of affection. "Luke knows more than most folks realize. If he says he can do it, I'm sure he can. Even so, a mangrove swamp is different from camping in Ohio."

Embarrassed, Luke looked at the floor while the biologist typed at the keyboard. Now on the computer screen was a satellite photo of Sanibel Island. The cursor zoomed in on

Dinkins Bay. The marina buildings and the lab's tin roof were familiar markers.

"I'm interested in those gravestones you found. I've lived here a long time, and it's not common to find graves in the mangroves. It happens, yeah. Especially if there's a shell mound in the area."

The man rolled his chair away from the computer to make room. "Point to the exact spot. Camping is illegal on most islands. They're wildlife preserves. We can't let you break the law."

Maribel stepped forward. She traced her finger along a narrow creek near the mouth of Dinkins Bay. The tiny island was in an area called Ladyfinger Lakes. It was a speck of high ground only a mile from the lab but screened from view by trees.

The biologist was suddenly more interested. It was as if he'd just had a good idea. "I know that little spot. Never went ashore like you kids did. It's not part of the preserve. And it's not an island. Not really."

"But there's water all around it," Maribel said.

"Sometimes, if the tide's high enough," Doc said. "See how it's connected to land by swamp? There used to be a shack back in there, near Woodring Road. Did you notice a cluster of pilings sticking up in the shallows? Big thick timbers, solid as stone."

Maribel said, "I did. Seven of them. They weren't marked with reflectors. I remember thinking it would be dangerous to run a boat in there at night."

"Good memory. Those pilings are all that's left of the shack. Bones Gate, people used to call it—maybe because so many boats hit them. Or could be there's a burial mound nearby. If so, stay away. They're protected by law. Plus, that's all private property. These days, no one goes back in there."

He zoomed the satellite view closer.

"Yep, that's the place. The lady who owned it was the first female fishing guide in Florida—one of the best in history. Her name was Esperanza Woodring. Esperanza was a great lady. She died a long time ago."

"Who owns it now?" Luke asked.

"Uh . . . let's just say an unusual woman. She lived in this area when she was a girl, then went away for a long, long time. No one knows where—almost like she disappeared, some claimed."

"Disappeared?" Luke didn't understand. "Ran away, you mean. Or maybe her folks moved."

Doc shook his head. "Years later the woman came back

and became a fishing guide. Folks thought that was a little strange, too. By then she was already in her sixties. But right away, she knew more about this area than just about anyone. The history, all the secret little islands. Kind of mysterious, really."

Luke paid closer attention.

The biologist explained, "Most people, it takes years to learn these waters. Not her. She ran daily charters until she had a stroke a while back. A blood clot in the brain."

Luke winced. His mother had died of a stroke.

Doc explained, "The woman recovered from the surgery faster than most, but she doesn't charter anymore. And she doesn't like visitors."

Maribel frowned. It was Doc's warning tone. "Is she . . . uh, mean?"

"Didn't used to be. But people can change as they age. Now she seldom speaks to anyone. Even me, she won't say more than a few words. Her name's Poinciana Wulfert. She has to be close to eighty years old now."

"That's kind of a weird name, isn't it?" Luke said. He was sounding it out in his head: *Poin-see-ANNA*.

"Poincianas are some of the most beautiful trees in the world. They bloom in summer," Doc told them. "Occasionally in the late fall, too. But that's rare. You've seen them—bright scarlet blossoms."

"Poinciana," Maribel repeated softly. "The woman's lucky to have such a nice name."

"She didn't think so," Doc said. "In the old days, tourists didn't like the idea of a hiring a woman fishing guide. So she went by her nickname—Pony Wulfert. It sounded more masculine than Poinciana, I guess. In private, though, she claimed she wasn't pretty enough to be named after such a beautiful tree. Either way, the nickname stuck."

"That's sad," Sabina said. "I want to meet her. Maybe you could call her on the phone."

Maribel sensed they were being tested when the biologist replied, "Doubt if she'd answer. She's what you might call reclusive. Do you know what that means?"

Sabina nodded. "It means she doesn't care what other people think. That's the way I'm going to be when I'm an adult."

Luke was thinking, *You already are.*

"Does she live alone?" Maribel asked.

"By choice," Doc said. "She grew up on an island near Sanibel before there were paved roads and electricity. She never did tell me exactly where. But she's as smart and tough as they come. A great storyteller, too—until she, uh, got sick. Captain Pony used to be a lot of fun."

"Then she'll love us," Sabina said. "We're fun, too."

The man liked the girl's confidence. "If you want to meet her, fine. This might be good for all of you. Pony still raises chickens and a pig or two, and catches fish. It can't be easy for someone her age. The thing is . . ." The man frowned, thinking about it.

"What's wrong?" Maribel wanted to know.

"Well, thing is, Pony Wulfert has a heck of a temper. And she's not afraid to speak her mind. She won't accept help from anyone. If a person stops by and offers, she runs them off her property. In the last few years, she's gotten sort of strange—out of loneliness, some say. Others blame her health problems."

"Runs them off how? Does she have a gun or something?" Luke asked.

The biologist chuckled. "I did hear a story about her chasing a salesman with a broom. Some claim it was a pitchfork, which I don't believe."

"A pitchfork?" Luke and Maribel didn't like the sound of that.

"Pony wouldn't need a pitchfork," Doc said. "She has something better—what islanders used to call an 'attack goose.' Trust me, a great big aggressive goose is enough to scare most people away."

Sabina was unfamiliar with the animal. "What is a goose?"

"*Un ganso*," Maribel translated.

"It's like a really big duck with a long neck," Luke added. "Never raised any, but I've seen them. Shoot, geese don't scare me one little bit."

The biologist chuckled. "Well, you'll find out. If you really want to camp there, you have to go to Captain Pony's house and ask for permission. All of you. In person. Do that, and I'll talk it over with Hannah, then speak to your mother."

"That's not fair," Sabina started to protest. But then her fingers found the blue-and-yellow shells of her necklace. Her eyes narrowed. "You *want* us to meet this old woman. And her giant *ganso*. Why? There has to be a reason."

Doc, who was kind and often quiet, also had a mysterious side. He ignored the question with a secretive shrug. His chair spun toward the computer and the photo of the Nile crocodile.

"First we need to know for sure what kind of crocodile is out there. If it's a Nile croc, you're not going anywhere near that place." He was about to say something else when his desk phone rang. With a wave, he requested privacy, saying, "That's my friend, the croc expert."

The kids wandered outside to the porch. Rain poured down off the tin roof. Thunder vibrated across the bay while a patch of clear sky promised the storm would soon pass. Pete thumped his tail once in greeting. The osprey was gone.

A few minutes later, Doc came out carrying something he'd drawn on a piece of paper. "My friend is pretty sure it's an American crocodile. When he has time, he'd like you kids to help him tag it for his records. Maybe in a few days, if he can get away."

"Tag a crocodile?" Luke said. He was grinning. "That thing has to be twelve feet long. Do you tag a croc the same way you tag sharks?"

"It's a little more complicated," the biologist said. "Don't worry about that now." He handed Maribel the paper. "Here's a map to Pony's house. It's not far. It's closer by boat, but it will be more polite if you ride bicycles to her front gate and ring the bell."

There was something else.

"That woman has a temper. And she's had some health problems, so mind your manners. Address her as Captain Pony. Or Ms. Wulfert. You could learn a lot from someone like Poinciana—if you can get past her goose."

SEVEN

HAUNTED BY A HEADLESS GHOST

Woodring Road was a dirt lane, with water on one side and mangrove trees, thick and gnarled, on the other. A gate blocked the entrance to a sandy stretch of beach. On the gate were warning signs in sloppy red paint:

> Keep Out!
> Beware of Goose!
> No Tourists Allowed!
> My Pig Bites!

Maribel stopped her bicycle and waited for the others

to catch up. "Wow, that's sort of a scary sign. Doc might have been right about that stroke affecting Ms. Wulfert's brain."

Once again, Luke winced at the mention of the woman's illness.

Beyond the gate was a dock. On a patch of sand was an old wooden house raised above the water on cones of pioneer concrete.

Immediately, Sabina made the connection with the grave markers they'd found.

Luke noted a bunch of chickens scratching in the yard. No sign of a big, mean goose. But there was a garden, with corn growing, and a fat pig sleeping in the shade.

On a dock at the water's edge, a person was trying to start the motor on a little green boat. It was a woman. She wore a baggy shirt, coveralls, and a ragged straw hat. Over and over, she yanked on the starter cord, but the little outboard only coughed and spit, and refused to run.

"Must be her," Maribel said. She cupped her hands and called, "Hello? Ma'am? Are you Captain Pony Wulfert? If you could use an extra set of hands, we'd like to help."

The woman looked up and glared. "Don't need nothin'

from a bunch of kids," she hollered back. "Go watch television or whatever it is you do on those little phones y'all yak on. I'm in a hurry."

Several more times, the old woman yanked on the starter rope. The motor chugged and sputtered, then died. She was getting tired. It was obvious from the way she rubbed her arm that her elbow hurt.

Maribel tried again. "We know a quite a bit about boats, ma'am. And Luke here's almost an expert when it comes to fixing engines."

Another icy glare was the response until Sabina spoke up. "It's true. We fish together a lot. And Luke grew up on a farm. He learned how to work on tractors and stuff. All sorts of small motors. Didn't you, Luke?"

The boy looked away while Captain Pony stood and wiped her hands on a towel. "Grew up on a farm, huh? There ain't no farms on this island. Haven't been since I was a child. First you interrupt my work. Now you're lying to me."

Luke cleared his throat. "A small farm in Ohio, not here," he said. "I'm no expert. But I might be able to get that motor running." He paused and remembered to add, "Ms. . . . uh, Captain . . . ma'am."

"Ohio, huh?" The woman walked toward the gate,

scattering a dozen chickens. She was tall but seemed taller because of her long strides and wide shoulders. It was hard to believe she was close to eighty years old. "You know something about farm animals and engines and such?"

The boy nodded. "A little."

Captain Pony flashed a frown. "Come to me tellin' stories, you best know more than a little. Answer this for me, and don't take time to make up a story—does a cow sleep standing up or lying down? If you really did live on a farm, you'll know."

Luke was startled. He wasn't good at tests. "Uh . . . a cow?"

"You heard me," the woman scoffed. "Kids today don't even know what a cow is."

"I raised a couple of Angus steers," Luke said. "They mostly slept lying down, I think." He paused to picture them in his head. "Yeah, with their front legs sort of folded under. When a cow gets up, it's always butt-first."

The woman hadn't expected the correct answer. But she wasn't convinced. "What about a horse?"

"Sleep, you mean? Standing up or lying down doesn't seem to matter to a horse."

"You sure?"

"Pretty sure," Luke said. "We had a Morgan gelding until it bit a chunk out of my stepfather."

This creased the old woman's face with what was almost a smile. "Hooray for the horse. The fool probably deserved it."

"He sure did," Luke agreed.

The woman seemed to like that, too. But she wasn't done. She gestured to the chickens that had scattered. Their red feathers looked metallic in the afternoon sunlight. "If you lived on a farm, you're bound to know what kinda chickens those are."

Sabina whispered, "Ask her about that mean goose."

Luke ignored her. "A bunch of little bantams, looks like to me. At the county fair, there were all types of breeds. I'm not gonna guess."

"Banties, we call them here," the woman corrected. "What color eggs they lay?"

"Brown, ma'am," Luke replied.

Captain Pony nodded but was still looking for an excuse not to open the gate. "Are you kids selling something? 'Cause if you are, just skedaddle yourselves out of here right now."

Maribel reached into her bag and produced one of the wild oranges. "We want to ask you about this. You know Dr. Ford, the biologist who lives next to the marina? He said this orange came from somewhere on your land. We found it this morning, but we couldn't find the tree."

"Marion Ford? *Doc* Ford?" The woman's scowl faded, then reappeared. "What were you kids doing snooping around my property? I don't tolerate trespassers. Where on my property?"

Maribel pointed bayside, where a halo of tall trees was visible above the mangroves. "Over there, I think. We thought it was an island. We didn't know you lived so close."

"When the tide's up, it is an island," the woman responded. "Bad things happen to people who go ashore there. Even me, I stay away. That there's your last warning."

"I bet I know why," Sabina said. "Because of the gravestones."

The old lady took a step back from the gate. Her face went pale. "You saw those?"

"I found them," Sabina replied. "One of the markers was decorated with little shells—a girl named Periwinkle. She was almost the same age as me when she died. Did you know her?"

The woman was so deep in thought, she didn't hear the question. Or didn't want to answer. Finally, her milky brown eyes seemed to clear. She refocused on Sabina. "You've got some sort of foreign accent. Where you from?"

The girl got off her bike. She used the kickstand and faced the old fishing guide, hands on her hips.

Luke recognized Sabina's stubborn expression and thought, *Uh-oh.*

"My sister and I don't have foreign accents," Sabina said tartly. "But almost everyone else in Florida does. We're from Cuba."

"Cuba." Captain Pony whispered the word as if it meant something to her. The first soft lines of a smile appeared. "Young lady, you got some fire in you. I like that. My daddy moved here from Cuba a long time ago. My family has lived and fished on these islands for a century."

"Do you speak Spanish?" The girl was hopeful.

The woman proved it by offering a warm Cuban welcome in Spanish to her "new little friend." After apologizing for her old-fashioned Havana accent, the woman switched back to English with a Southern twang.

"Two little Cuban girls," she said. "Makes sense you were the one to find those graves."

Sabina's quizzical expression asked, *What do you mean?*

"Chosen by them that's buried there, maybe," the woman said in a spooky way. After a few seconds of thought, she nodded. "Yep. Has to be. Folks ever tell you that everything in this world happens for a reason? Well, that there is pure donkey dung. Bad things happen to good folks every day. But it is true that, when the timing's just right, people sometimes meet for a reason. Don't ask me how I know. But I do."

Captain Pony stared into Sabina's face. "Cuba, yeah, I can see it. You've got a light of the magic ladies in your eyes. The *santeras*. You know about them?"

"The women dressed in white," Sabina replied. "Yes, they liked me. I'd sneak away from home and they'd teach me things."

The old fishing guide nodded her approval. "I bet they did. You wouldn't have found those graves otherwise. In all my years here, no one has bothered to care. Or had the nerve. Being who you are, you'll understand—that island you found? It's haunted."

Sabina felt honored. "That is so cool. Dead people choose me all the time. Haunted how? By the dead girl, you think?"

"By an Indian king," the woman replied.

This was a surprising thing to hear. But Pony Wulfert was serious.

"That's right, a king used to live there—until Spanish explorers cut off his head. That was five hundred years ago. Now the king's ghost has come back and is causing me nothing but . . ." Her voice faded when she noticed the strange look she was getting from Luke.

"Stop your gawking," she muttered. "I might have had brain surgery, but I'm not bat-daft loco."

Crazy, she meant.

"Of course you're not, ma'am," Maribel said.

Luke didn't agree but nodded anyway.

"Even if you are," Sabina said, "who cares? People say I'm crazy all the time."

The woman made a coughing sound, trying not to laugh. "I'm starting to believe that's true about both of us. But I got no time to stand around jawing with a bunch of young'uns. I got a mess of mullet to smoke, and wood to chop—and that dang little motor of mine's busted. Already said I'm in a hurry, sweetie."

"I'm not sweet. And we're not young'uns—whatever those are," Sabina countered politely.

"It's an old country expression," the woman explained. "Sweetie, sugar—it's the way we talk." She added, with an edge, "There are worse things to call a child with a sharp tongue."

"Anyway, ghosts love me," Sabina insisted.

"They do, huh?" This time the old fishing guide didn't bother to hide her smile.

"Yes, ma'am. I see them lots of times when I walk in my sleep."

"Walk in your . . . for true?" Fascinated, the woman took a step closer.

The girl nodded as if proud of herself.

"I'll be doggone," the old lady said. "There's something else we got in common. Many a time I've woken up standing in the water, or some field. Never remembered leaving my bed."

"Isn't it fun?" Sabina replied. "Let us look for that orange tree. We'll help do whatever work you need done—except smoke a fish. I hate smoking. But we're experts at just about everything else."

Captain Wulfert laughed aloud while Maribel added, "I can explain why we're looking for wild orange trees, ma'am. While we're talking, though, why not at least let Luke try to start that motor? If you're in a hurry, we're wasting time."

The woman agreed, but something bothered her. Her focus shifted to Luke. "You're an expert on motors, huh? That's hard to believe, a young fella your age. Mind if I ask a few more questions?"

The boy took a deep breath. He readied himself for another test.

There was no guessing what kind of questions this strange old lady might ask.

EIGHT
A BROKEN MOTOR AND A MYSTERIOUS MAN

Captain Pony told Sabina there would be no more talk about ghosts or the Native American king until she was convinced that Luke knew something about outboard motors. She put her large, sun-browned hands on the gate and addressed the boy. "I've yet to meet a fella who didn't claim to be a mechanic. Most aren't worth a flip. I earn my living from that little boat. Can't risk you damaging my engine worse than it already is. Tell me the truth or turn those bikes around and go home."

Luke shifted from foot to foot. He scratched at the burn scar hidden beneath his navy-blue T-shirt. "I'm no expert," he said again. "If I can't figure out what's wrong, I'll tell you. But I'll need some tools."

"You don't think I know that?" the woman snapped. "What kind?"

"Well, a screwdriver and a spark-plug wrench . . . or a set of ratchets. If you've got one of those small voltage testers, that would be good, too."

Sabina interrupted, "Maribel can help figure it out. She knows more about boats than most adults. That's what Dr. Ford says, and it's true."

Captain Pony's eyes sparked for an instant. "Well, I guarantee Marion Ford wasn't including me in that discussion. Doubt if there's a person alive knows these waters or boats better than me."

"Doc said that, too," Maribel added. "That we could learn a lot from you, if you'd give us a chance."

The compliment softened the woman's face. She paused and folded the towel she held. "Well, heaven knows, I could use some help around this place. But I'm gonna warn you right now, I can't pay much. Truth is"—the woman seemed embarrassed—"I can't pay you nothing until the end of the month. Money don't come as easy these days as it used to."

Maribel sensed that the old lady was weary—and that she was worried about something else. Something serious. "We don't expect to be paid," the girl said, and explained why they were searching for old orange trees.

As they talked, Luke's sharp eyes noticed that weeds were taking over the yard. Bits of junk were scattered around. There were scraps of good lumber, too.

More interesting was a battered old refrigerator in the corner of the yard. It had been converted into a meat smoker by adding a chimney. A metal box was clamped to its side. In Ohio, he and his Little League pals had made a similar grill from a fifty-five-gallon barrel. It was their coach's favorite way to cook.

The boy waited for an opening to ask, "What's the best wood to use, you think, for curing meat with wood smoke?" He motioned to the refrigerator.

"Buttonwood," the woman replied without hesitating. "A big ol' buttonwood tree grows down by my dock. Biggest around that I've seen. Been trimming the limbs for years— which is why I make the best smoked mullet you ever tasted."

Luke nodded his appreciation. "If I get your motor started, maybe we could do a sort of trade. In return, you teach me how to smoke mullet. And let us look for that orange tree.

I've cooked chicken and pork ribs in a smoker, but never fish. Seems like fish would get mushy and fall apart."

No doubt about it now: Captain Pony Wulfert was impressed.

She eyed the boy as if he were a pleasant oddity. "Not if you do it right," she said. "Guess I'd be willing to teach you a few more secrets I've learned along the way."

Luke surveyed the yard. "And that lumber needs to be covered with a tarp before it rots. Or moved to one of those sheds. It wouldn't take us much time."

The old woman was convinced. She pulled the gate open and stepped aside. "Okay, then. If a little hard work don't bother you kids none, come on in. Truth is, my eyes ain't what they used to be. I wasted most the day looking for an animal of mine that run off. Or got stolen, maybe—or worse. That's why I'm in a hurry. I've got to get that motor started and go looking."

Captain Pony was walking toward the water where her green boat was tied. Nearby was a battered canoe and the gnarled old buttonwood tree.

Sabina trotted to catch up. "What do you mean, stolen, or worse? What kind of animal? A dog?"

"A big white goose named Carlos," the woman replied.

"She's smarter than any dog you've ever met. Meaner, too. Couple days ago, my new neighbor threatened to kill her. That's why I'm so worried."

"Your neighbor? That's terrible."

"Oh, he is a skunk-in-the-weeds," Captain Pony replied. "Him and some other fella just built a big ugly house about a mile down the shore. Wanted to buy my property, too. But I wouldn't sell. Carlos has chased that joker off my land more than once. Which is why the man—"

A wild, distant honking caused the woman to go silent. Squawks and hisses were mixed in.

The old fishing guide turned to the kids, her expression helpless. "That's her, Carlos! My goose is in trouble. I can tell by the sound of her bugle calls."

After a glance at the useless boat, Captain Pony took several stumbling steps in an attempt to rush to the goose's rescue. But she was too old to run.

"We'll go," Maribel hollered. She sprinted away, followed by Sabina and Luke.

The shrill honking sounds came from a larger body of water beyond the mangroves—San Carlos Bay.

Carlos. The same name as the goose. The coincidence—if it was a coincidence—didn't cross Maribel's mind until her long legs had carried her through the mangroves to the water's edge.

In the distance was a fancy dock, newly built. A sleek yellow cabin cruiser with four outboard motors was tied there. It was the size of a deluxe RV bus. For an instant, a goose appeared near the dock. It was being chased by a tall, skinny man about to swing a bat . . . or an ax. The bird turned and disappeared behind some the trees. The skinny man rushed in pursuit.

Sabina saw it happening, too, and ran faster. Instead of following Maribel along the shore, she cut through a clump of bushes and came out on a dirt road. The road tunneled through the mangroves for a hundred yards. Around a curve was an industrial-sized gate. Beyond was an asphalt drive and a huge, ugly concrete house.

Chest heaving, the girl stopped and peered through the gate's metal bars. The skinny man, with his back to her, held an ax, ready to swing it. He had the goose trapped against a small, strange-looking building. Strange because it had a roof and a heavy metal door, but no windows.

"Leave Carlos alone!" the girl threatened. "We'll call the police and they'll arrest you!"

She didn't expect what happened next. The man stiffened with surprise. It was as if he was afraid of the police. Without turning around, he dropped the ax and ran to the house.

The goose charged after the man, honking furiously. The bird bit the guy several times on the legs before he got the door open and escaped inside. His screams were high-pitched yips.

"Carlos!" Sabina hollered. "Come on. Fly away before he changes his mind."

The goose heard the girl. Instead of flying, it galloped toward her, wings spread wide. There was an electric whirring noise. The heavy gate began to slide open. Maybe someone inside the house had pushed a button.

Sabina wondered about that until Carlos was closer. The bird was taller than she was. It had a long snakelike neck, an orange beak, and legs as thick as tree limbs. It was honking as if mad at her for some reason.

"Whoa—I'm your friend," the girl called. She began backing away, hands outstretched. "Stop! Slow down. I just saved your life, you dumb bird!"

The goose was almost to the gate. It hadn't slowed a step.

Sabina whirled around and ran.

NINE

BITTEN ON THE BUTT
BY A GOOSE

Luke was twenty steps behind Maribel, almost to the dock and the concrete house, when Sabina sprinted out of the trees and turned toward him

"Hey . . . what's wrong?" he yelled.

"Run for your life," she called in a panic. "That stupid bird just bit me on the butt!"

Maribel heard her, too.

By then Luke could see the goose. It was chasing the girl. Every few steps, it would lunge and nip at her backside.

"Ouch . . . ouch!" Sabina shrieked.

She lurched forward. She covered her backside with her

hands and kept running. Luke recognized some of the sharp curse words she added in Spanish.

The goose responded with hisses and snapped at her again.

Luke started laughing. He couldn't help himself. It was hilarious—at first. But then Sabina raced past him. Suddenly the boy was face-to-face with a goose that had to be four feet tall.

The giant bird slowed. Tiny black eyes glittered. They shifted to Luke.

Honk-hiss—honk-honk-hiss. The orange beak clattered like bones clacking. The goose's trumpeting changed to a shrill shriek.

Carlos pumped her head up and down like an angry bull, then lowered her beak to the sand. The goose charged.

Luke was no longer laughing. He backed a few steps, then stopped. In Ohio, he had learned how to deal with aggressive farm dogs. No matter the breed, their job was to protect their owner's property and chase off intruders.

They weren't mean dogs—usually. They didn't want to fight, or even bite. Most of them wanted an excuse to be friendly.

Maybe the same was true of this angry "attack goose."

The boy stood his ground. He threw his arms wide to make himself appear larger. He maintained eye contact—animals considered eye contact intimidating. Carlos used her wings to stop. Her shrill trumpeting changed to a series of loud warning honks.

Luke spoke softly, saying, "Hey . . . it's okay. I'm not going to hurt you. Relax." He continued to make calming sounds while he backed away.

The goose followed as if unsure what to do.

Maribel was jogging toward them. Her face showed concern. "Do you need help? Should I get a stick or something? That goose is loco."

Luke shook his head. He put a finger to his lips and motioned toward the bushes, meaning, *Go around us.*

Reluctantly, Maribel circled into the mangroves, yet she continued to watch in case she was needed. By then Sabina was halfway to Captain Pony's house, and still running hard.

Luke whispered, "Carlos . . . Carlos . . . such a nice little goose. Yes, you are." He said this over and over, barely moving his lips.

The bird's warning honks softened into a string of quacks and clacking beak noises.

The boy began to relax. He stared at the bird and

continued to whisper comforting thoughts. "Let's go home. That's a good boy . . . girl, I mean. Yep . . . no need to bite me on the butt. You're safe now."

That seemed to be true until a gravelly voice from the sleek cabin cruiser threatened them. "You nosy kids stay away from here! I'll shoot that duck if it ever comes near my house again! Tell that crazy old lady what I said!"

The cabin cruiser was huge, with a gleaming chrome tower. Atop the tower was a large man, not the skinny guy who'd had been chasing the bird with an ax. It was hard to tell much more because of the hooded rain jacket the man wore.

Luke felt his face flush and made a big mistake. He glared and shouted, "If you don't know the difference between a goose and a duck, that's your problem, mister! And Captain Pony's not crazy. You'd better leave them both alone."

The big man swore and shouted, "I don't care if it's a freakin' swan. I'll cut that bird up and feed it to my snakes."

Snakes?

Luke didn't have time to think about it. All the yelling had upset the bird again. Carlos leaped around, wings flapping, and waddled toward the guy at high speed, determined to attack.

The boy raced after the bird. Maribel came out of the

trees to help. They were gaining on the creature when, from high above, a silver shadow swooped down. The shadow collided with Carlos so hard, the giant goose skidded onto her side in shock.

Luke heard a familiar whistling call. He looked up and searched the blue sky above.

Peep-peep-pee! SAR-SRR-SARR, screamed the silver shadow.

It was the osprey. The way the fish hawk soared high, tilting to the left and then the right, it resembled a fighter jet in a movie.

The goose wasn't hurt. But she was exhausted after so much excitement. She lay in the sand, gasping for air. The boy knelt and stroked the animal's back. When the osprey threatened to dive-bomb them again, he stood and waved the bird away.

"We're friends, so knock it off!" he hollered. "Same as the dog."

Then Luke did a silly thing. He pointed to the man who was still yelling threats from the boat.

"Attack!" the boy whispered without moving his lips.

The osprey fluttered in midair. Its whistling chirps resembled the notes of a screaming teapot. Then it rocketed toward the big fancy boat.

Maribel put her hand to her mouth in disbelief at what happened next. For an instant, the large man froze, then leaped out of the speeding bird's path. There was a growling howl. He stumbled, fell, and hit the water with a heavy splash.

"L-Luke," the girl stammered. "What just happened? It was almost like that osprey was protecting us."

The boy rubbed at the lightning scar on his shoulder. "Maybe," he mumbled. "Did that jerk say something about snakes?"

"Sounded like it," Maribel said. She waited to confirm that the man could swim before demanding, "What about that osprey? I'm starting to believe you can talk to animals."

"Anyone can talk to animals," Luke said. "Doesn't mean they'll listen."

The boy squatted beside the goose and helped her to her feet.

"Come on, Carlos," he said. "If you don't want to get fed to a snake, you better follow us home."

TEN
NO-SEE-UMS AND BAT HOUSES

When Sabina saw the giant white bird waddling calmly beside Luke, she said to Captain Pony, "I wish the Spaniards who cut off the king's head could meet your goose. I wonder how they would get along?"

That was what they'd been talking about—the headless ghost the old lady had mentioned earlier. Not that Captain Pony was eager to discuss the subject.

"Folks already think I'm touched in the noggin," the woman confided. "Nobody believes in ghosts these days. And I shouldn't be filling your head with nonsense. The only reason I told you is . . . well, you're friends with those magic women in Cuba. In fact, there's sorta somethin' different about every one of you kids."

Captain Pony looked from Luke to Sabina as she thought about it.

"Yep, different. Has to be. Periwinkle wouldn't let you find her grave if there wasn't a reason. And my goose don't like no one except me and my chickens. I hatched Carlos from an egg. But there she is, following that boy like a pet dog. What's his name again?"

Scowling, Sabina said, "Your goose bit me on the butt and it hurt. Now those two are just showing off to make me mad. The farm boy's name is Luke."

"You got a smart-aleck attitude, young lady." The old fishing guide was smiling. "Don't blame that farmer Luke one bit. Think he can fix my boat?"

"If Luke can't, my sister can. She's almost as smart as me," the girl responded. "If we help, will you tell us more about the ghost of the dead king?"

Amused, the woman said again, "*Different.* Yes, you kids are. I can't remember the last time I had a reason to laugh. Reckon it might be a good thing to have you three hang around for a while and help out—if your mama says it's okay."

"She will," Sabina said. "Don't worry, you can talk all you want about ghosts. At the marina where we live, adults don't believe anything I say anyway."

The remark got another peal of soft laughter.

They were standing on the beach by the little green boat. The recent storm had washed the air clean. Mangroves painted the bay with waxen shadows where fish jumped. Pelicans crashed the water nearby. It was late afternoon, an hour before sunset.

When the goose saw the old lady, it honked a greeting and came at her on the run.

"Don't be afraid," Captain Pony told Sabina. "Carlos and I don't get many visitors. She'll warm up to you." Stroking the bird's neck, she confided, "The way my new neighbor's been acting, we could use another set of eyes around here. That skunk-in-the-weeds is a thief. Broke into my house, I think, and stole something from me."

"You should go to the police! What did he steal?"

The woman touched a finger to her lips to keep it a secret.

"When the time's right, I'll tell you, sugar." She glanced in the direction of the big cement house. "That joker might be dangerous, too, from what you said about that ax."

Luke was relieved when Captain Pony said, "It appears you know how to use a wrench," and left him alone to work on the little boat's outboard motor.

Someone looking over his shoulder made the boy nervous. He was more likely to screw up, break a tool in some dumb way, or whack his own thumb with a hammer.

It had been like that with his stepfather on the farm. And it had gotten worse, three years ago, after his mother's funeral.

He was thinking about that when the old lady's voice grabbed his attention. "You girls help me get a fire started," she called to Maribel and Sabina. "The bugs will be eatin' us alive now it's almost sunset. And we've got mullet to catch and smoke."

When Sabina insisted, "I'll gather wood, but I'm not smoking anything," Luke rolled his eyes. He liked the girls. Having irritating sisters was fun sometimes.

True, there were things about Ohio he missed—his Little League teammates, the smell of baling hay in summer, and the sweet maple odor of autumn leaves. But he did not miss that tense feeling in his stomach, the daily fear of doing something dumb.

Florida had become home.

Luke leaned over the little motor and went to work. The old lady had provided tools. And she wasn't exaggerating about the bugs. He swatted at them while removing and cleaning the spark plugs. He checked the plug wires for spark. A tiny screw beneath the fuel filter released a stream of water that shouldn't have been there.

Water in the fuel line, the boy thought. *That's the problem.*

He was right. After three yanks on the starter cord, the motor clattered to life.

"Hooray for you, Luke boy," Captain Pony whooped, and waved her thanks.

She and the sisters were on chairs near a smoldering campfire. Behind them, the old refrigerator was spouting smoke, too. Inside, splits of mullet were being cooked and cured by glowing chunks of buttonwood. The fish was freshly cleaned but not skinned.

"Get over here out of the bugs," the woman urged. "This smudge we lit will keep them away." She glanced up at the massive old tree near the shoreline. "That's something else buttonwood is good for."

By then, Luke's arms looked like someone had sprinkled them with black pepper. The bugs were tiny gnats called no-see-ums. Their bites felt like drops of acid on his skin.

He shut off the engine and hurried across the beach to an empty chair.

"You have any bug spray, ma'am? These no-see-ums are tearing me up."

"Sand flies, we call 'em," the old lady said. "Them chemicals are bad for a person. And the junk sprays they sell in stores don't work. Summer or winter, you kids need to wear long sleeves and pants this time of day. For now, though, try this."

She handed the boy a bottle of something that looked like cough syrup. But it smelled good. Kind of spicy.

"What is it?"

"Witch-hazel oil," the woman said. She explained that just about any kind of body oil stopped sand flies if you put it on thick enough. Mud worked, too, when you were desperate. In the old days they had used oil made from the stumps of pine trees. "Lighter pine," they'd called the wood. It contained so much sap, a stick would burn like a torch.

"Witch-hazel oil is easier," she continued. "And a lot safer. To make pine oil, we had to put wood in a can and bury it in a fire. Go ahead, rub some on your arms and ankles. When the sand flies land, they get stuck in the witch hazel and can't bite."

Luke did as he was told. Soon he was comfortable again. He sat listening to the girls and the old fishing guide talk. The flames of the campfire brightened in the slow sunset dusk. Maribel had already phoned home. There was no rush to get back to the marina.

The boy felt good about getting the little motor started. Captain Pony had shown confidence in him. That was a nice feeling, too. He wanted to ask about the racks of fish cooking in the smoker. But Maribel kept the woman busy with questions about what it had been like to live in Florida without electricity or air-conditioning. And Sabina wanted to hear about the headless ghost.

The girls were still determined to camp out on the island. Luke was thinking about that when he noticed an odd-looking birdhouse bolted high in a nearby tree. Orange sunset light showed that the front panel had been decorated with the silhouette of a . . . what?

He got up and walked toward the thing. At the same instant, a whirlpool of squeaking leathery creatures exited the structure and flew skyward. He didn't need to get any closer to recognize the design carved there long ago.

"A bat house," he said. "Those are bats."

"Dozens of them sleep there all day," Captain Pony

responded. "At sunset they fly out to feed. A bat will eat its weight in mosquitoes and other pests in a single night. That's another trick we learned in the old days. Didn't need poison to kill skeeters. Built that bat house myself when I was no older than you kids. You like my carving?"

Luke was impressed. "I had a wood-burning set once, but I'm not much of an artist. I'd like to make one of those bat houses. Can you show me how?"

"Maybe we could sell them," Maribel suggested to the woman. "I didn't know bats ate mosquitoes. Everyone in Florida should have a place for them to live. It might be a good way for you to make money."

Captain Pony was surprised by the idea. But her response was stopped by a muffled, thunderous growl. Then a series of grunts.

The kids knew right away it was the saltwater crocodile. The old lady didn't. Frightened, she hunkered low in the flickering light of the fire.

"You hear that?" she whispered.

The children nodded. "Sure we do," said Maribel.

"Thank goodness!" Relieved, the woman took a deep breath. "Last couple of weeks, I thought I was losing my mind. That's him, the ghost—King Carlos."

Sabina jumped up from her chair. "Carlos? Where? I thought that stupid goose was in the pen with the chickens."

It was several seconds before the woman spoke. "I'm talking about the king who ruled most of South Florida until him and a bunch of his people were killed by the Spaniards. Carlos wasn't the king's real name. It was Caalus or something similar, but the Spaniards wrote it down wrong or couldn't pronounce it. Since I was a girl, every rooster and goose I've ever raised has been named Carlos out of respect for the people who lived here."

Her head swiveled toward a pyramid of distant trees. "The place you kids found those oranges. Do you remember a ring of seven old pilings sticking out of the water?"

Maribel nodded. "Dr. Ford told us. He called it . . ." She had to think for a moment. "He called it Bones Gate. A lot of boats have crashed there, he said."

"A few. Not a lot. But that's not the real story," the woman replied. "No one remembers anymore, but that little spot you found is a sacred place—Bonefield Key, we called it. There was a little shack built next to it. That's how those old pilings got the name. On the full moon, some say, that gate opens only one way. And some folks never find their way back."

Another low growl reached them from across the water.

Captain Pony's face went pale. "His ghost," she whispered. "Every night for weeks I've heard that awful sound. Carlos has come back to torment me—and I know why."

Maribel didn't have the courage to say what slipped easily from her sister's mouth.

"Did you do something to offend the king?" Sabina asked. "There has to be a reason."

"Of course not," the woman snapped. "And it's none of your business if I did."

"Then you've got nothing to worry about," Sabina assured her. "Besides, that isn't a ghost. It's a crocodile. Or, until someone proves me wrong, a dragon."

The old lady's eyes widened. "A crocodile? There ain't been no crocs around here for years. And sure enough no dragons. What makes you say such a silly thing?"

Sabina plopped back down in her chair. "Tell us about King Carlos. *Please?* If you do, I'll tell you why I'm sure that's not a ghost punishing you for whatever you did to make him mad."

ELEVEN
THE GOLD MEDALLION

The campfire popped. Sparks twirled into the sunset sky. Captain Pony sat back and told them what Florida had been like when Spanish explorers arrived more than five hundred years ago.

"These islands belonged to a fierce people called the Calusa. Remember me saying the king's real name was Caalus? Well, at least least they got the name of his people close to right. They built shell mounds along this coast for hundreds of miles. Not as big as the pyramids in Egypt, but similar in shape, some claim. A whole kingdom of mounds and canals and fancy courtyards. The Calusa were big men and women. They were so much taller than the Spaniards, the Spaniards thought they had sailed into a land ruled by giants."

Ca-LOO-sah? Luke repeated the name in his head. He glanced at Maribel. They both wondered if the story was true.

"Oh, it's true all right," the woman said, as if reading their minds. "When I was a fishing guide, some of my clients were Calusa experts. Archaeologists. They hired me to boat 'em around the islands so they could study what the Calusa people left behind. Even forty years ago, most of their mounds were already gone. Dug up to make roads and such. That big house my new neighbor built? Used to be a mound there, too."

"That skunk-in-the-weeds," Sabina said bitterly. "No wonder your goose doesn't like him."

Pony smiled. In her gnarled hand was a jar of iced sweet tea. She sipped at the tea and decided to share a detail she'd never shared with anyone. After a nod in the direction of the bay, she said, "But I never took them—or anyone else—to the spot you kids found."

"Why not if they were archaeologists?" Maribel asked. "Luke found a shell tool out there. And mounds—we saw them. Archaeologists might have discovered something important about the Calusa."

Captain Pony sniffed and sighed. "I was wrong. I know that now. The time will come when I'll call in modern experts. Maybe even donate the land so greedy fools won't build condos and such." She took another sip of sweet tea. "But folks are buried there. It's a private place. Far as I know, you kids are the first to explore the Bone Tunnel since I was a little girl."

Sabina was confused. "I thought you called it Bonefield Key."

"You're a sharp one, you are. Most called it Bonefield Key," the woman said. "In my mind, though, it's the Bone Tunnel. And I've got my reasons."

Sabina wasn't satisfied. "We didn't see any bones *or* a tunnel. We walked all over that island."

"Oh, there's a tunnel there all right," the woman said in a whisper. "Just not the type you're picturing. That's all I have to say on the matter."

"Like a cave, you mean?" the girl asked.

Captain Pony shook her head no, then changed the subject. "I don't doubt your story about a saltwater crocodile. But that doesn't explain other sounds I've heard late at night. Animal noises. Crying and grunts and groans and howling like wild dogs."

"Could be coyotes," Luke put in. "They come around the marina sometimes. I've seen them."

"Maybe," the woman said, nodding. "But have you ever used a shovel to dig through shells? That's something else I've heard the last week or so. Like metal scraping a blackboard. It's a sound you don't forget. I lie awake sometimes, wondering if someone isn't digging up a grave." She paused. "Or trying to dig their way out."

Maribel felt an electric sensation on her neck. Goose bumps. "Maybe your new neighbor is trying to scare you. You said he's mad because you won't sell your land."

"No human could make the noises I've heard," Captain Pony replied. She took another drink of her tea. "Your friend, Dr. Ford, will think I'm plumb crazy for talking about ghosts. But the story about the Calusa king is true. One of the scientists put it in a book. So there's no harm, I guess, in telling you what's written in history. You kids can decide for yourselves."

The Calusa were different from some Native tribes, the woman explained. They had a king, not a tribal chief. When the Spaniards arrived, King Carlos ruled most of what is now South Florida. The invaders, even with their steel swords and armor, couldn't defeat the Calusa in battle. So they came up with a plot to murder the king.

Leaning toward the fire, Pony touched a finger to her forehead. "Carlos wore a gold medal—a medallion—right here to show he was king of all this land. It was small, covered with strange designs. I've got a book in the house if you want to see a drawing. After the Spaniards murdered Carlos, they cut off his head. Could be I'm wrong about the details. My memory ain't what it used to be."

"His head? That's just sick," Maribel said. "To get the gold medallion?"

"They were afraid of the king's magic powers, in my opinion," the woman said. "The Spaniards had a priest on their ship. In his journal he wrote that, at night, King Carlos went to where his ancestors were buried and talked to the dead. The dead told him things about the future that came true. Could be that Carlos scared the Spaniards, so they killed him. But they didn't take the medallion. Maybe that scared them, too."

"The king had psychic powers." Sabina said this as if she'd known it all along. "So do I. That's why ghosts like me."

The woman gave the girl a searching look. Her dark eyes glittered above the flames of the campfire. "I wouldn't be a bit surprised, sugar. You wouldn't have found those graves if you didn't have a special gift of some type."

"I have lots of special gifts," Sabina agreed. "Are you sure the Spaniards didn't take the medallion? Those invaders were bad. If they were killers, they were probably thieves, too."

In a flat tone, the old fishing guide replied, "Yep. I'm pretty sure it's still somewhere on my property. I wish someone would find it and stop fools from digging up those mounds. The only gold the Calusa had was from a Spanish coin or two. Those jokers are destroying history and wasting their time. Breaking the law, too!"

"But how can you be sure those murderers didn't take the medallion?" Sabina pressed.

Captain Pony scratched her forehead. She stared at the fire while insects churred a violin chorus from the trees. Finally, she spoke. "Here's another part of the story. You three will be the first to hear it in a long, long time. There was a little girl who lived on an island not far from here. She had a special gift. Same as you."

Luke's attention had drifted until then. He began to listen closely.

The local girl had a gift for finding unusual things, the woman explained. More than fifty years ago, while digging a garden, she had found the gold medallion. Buried with the

96

medallion was a human skull, and a bunch of colorful glass beads.

The Spaniards called them chevron beads. The invaders had brought the beads to trade with the Native people. Other trade items included the first orange seeds to arrive in Florida.

Maribel sat straighter. She wanted to ask if there was a connection with the Spaniards and the oranges she, Sabina, and Luke had found. Instead she waited politely while the woman continued to talk.

"At the time, the little girl didn't know she'd dug up the skull of the great King Carlos. Even so, she reburied it out of respect. But she got greedy. She took the gold medallion and the beads and snuck them home to her room."

"That's bad luck," Sabina said. After thinking about it, though, she added, "Sounds like something I would do. Are you sure this isn't a story someone made up?"

"Oh, it's true as true can be," the old fishing guide said. She snapped a twig and tossed it into the flames. "Poor, scared little thing didn't tell a soul. Kept it all a secret until she started having terrible dreams. Nightmares. Got worse and worse. Her parents feared she was losing her mind. The girl got so scared she ran away—disappeared, some said. When her folks finally found her, the girl claimed she took the medallion back and buried it with the skull."

"Was it Periwinkle?" Sabina was referring to the name on the gravestone. "Did her bad dreams ago away?"

"Maybe—unless greed got the best of her," the woman answered, getting up from her chair. She grunted and stretched the way old people did when their backs hurt. A peach-colored halo over the bay meant the sun had just set. "It'll be dark soon," Pony continued. "Come on. I'll walk you to the gate. You kids got lights on your bicycles?"

Sabina didn't want to leave. "We have lights and plenty of time. Please finish the rest of your story. Is King Carlos buried out there?" She pointed toward the island. "Is that why you call it the Bone Tunnel?"

Rather than answer, the old lady changed the subject and led them away from the fire. Luke received another compliment for fixing her outboard motor. They were all invited back tomorrow to help clean up her property or learn how to cook fish in a smoker.

"It was years ago that I built that bat house," she added with a laugh. "We can try that, too, if you want. Guess I could use the extra money. All I do now is sell a few smoked mullet and bait to fishermen to pay my bills."

Maribel had waited politely long enough. At the gate, she spoke up. "Finding that orange tree is important, ma'am. Would you mind if we went back and looked for it? We've even discussed camping there for a few nights—if you'll let us."

Captain Pony didn't seem surprised at all by the request. "I've been thinking about that. Those noises I mentioned don't scare you?"

Maribel replied, "If they do, we could pack up and leave real fast. We'd have a rental boat from the marina. A VHF radio, too."

"Got it all planned out, do you?" The woman mulled it over. "Well, bless your little heart. Anybody else, I'd say no. But you kids were allowed to find that spot for a reason. Same way you found me—and helped save Carlos from that nasty neighbor of mine." A sweet sadness crept into Pony's voice. "Truth is, at my age, there ain't a lot of time left for having fun. So why not?"

The girls clapped their hands.

"Not so fast." The old fishing guide was no longer smiling. She glanced skyward. A big milky moon was visible despite the sunset afterglow. That seemed to make up her mind.

"Should be okay for the next few weeks," she said. "But you start by setting up camp next to my house, where I can keep an eye on you. There's a lot you need to learn about camping in the mangroves—or before you risk a night all alone out there."

Bonefield Key she meant.

As the kids were mounting their bikes, the old fishing guide took Sabina aside and added a private warning in Spanish. "Listen to me! Never camp there on a full moon unless I say it's okay," she whispered. "You've got to promise."

Since they were sharing secrets, the girl felt it was okay to call the woman by her real name. "I promise. But why, Poinciana?"

"Don't call me that." The woman bristled. "A tree as pretty as a poinciana don't fit a person with my looks. That's why, early on, folks started calling me Pony."

Instead of shrinking back, Sabina looked into the old lady's eyes. "You're a lot prettier than I'll be at your age. I know it—and I don't care. You can trust me, Poinciana. What's so dangerous about the Bone . . ." The girl hesitated before saying, "The Bone *Tunnel*?"

The old lady cleared her throat, suddenly emotional. "You are so wrong, my new little friend. You're a beautiful young person. Just do as I say, child. Maybe one day I'll tell you the truth about what can happen out there"—Captain Pony looked toward the water—"when the moon is full. The ancient people who lived here still have ancient secrets. If the Calusa want you to know, they will you show you the way. "

TWELVE
SCORPIONS AND AN ANCIENT SHELL HORN

Maribel and Sabina had never heard of Halloween until they left Cuba and arrived in the United States.

The sisters hadn't believed the stories at first. To Sabina, Halloween sounded too wonderful to be true. Kids could dress up like witches or ghosts, and wander the streets at night eating free candy?

But it was true.

In Florida, no excuses were needed. There would be no weird looks from strangers like those Sabina had received after sneaking into the beautiful cemetery west of Havana. Those looks might have had something to do with the black cloak she'd worn out of respect.

That was a long time ago, of course. Back when she was a little kid.

There was a lot to like about living here. There were things to dislike, too. But Sabina loved Halloween. In a thousand years, she couldn't have thought of a more perfect way to celebrate the day before her birthday.

Sabina was thinking about that on Wednesday when they rode their bikes to Captain Pony's house. Every day after school this week, the kids had worked in the yard. They had found a spot on the beach where they could build a place to camp. And they had already learned a lot about how Florida's first settlers had survived, despite the heat and bugs.

"Let the dead rest in peace," the old fishing guide said that afternoon when the trio arrived. "Today, no more questions about the gold medallion or that poor young girl. *Please?* Upsets me too much to even think about."

Sabina heard that sweet, sad tone again. Maribel heard it, too.

"We need to do something to cheer Pony up," Maribel suggested to Luke. "I'm worried about her health. Or maybe it's because she's low on money. Has to be awful to be old and poor."

"It's not a lot of laughs at our age, either," the boy replied, tightening his leather gloves. He had been collecting lumber to build their first bat house. "Hey—take a look at this. I've got an idea."

"About what?"

"About how to cheer up the old lady. See for yourself."

Sabina drifted closer and watched him kick over a board. Beneath the board was a scorpion, five inches long. Its body was covered with what looked like black armor. Startled by the sunlight, the scorpion thrust its pincers upward as a warning. At the end of its curly tail was a needle, sharp as a thorn.

"Don't mess with that," Maribel said. She took a step back. "Even through your gloves, it could sting you. We saw lots of scorpions in Cuba. They're not deadly, but they sure hurt. I know. I stepped on one once."

"That woodpile is loaded with them," the boy replied. "Dozens, some with hundreds of babies on their bellies. Last night, I looked up scorpions on the computer. In some parts of the world, yeah, they're really dangerous. But these are no worse than a wasp sting. I can't wait to tell Captain Pony the good news."

Sabina wrinkled her nose with disgust. "If you think a woodpile full of scorpions will make Poinciana happy, please don't choose a birthday present for me." As an aside, she whispered to her sister in Spanish, "He falls down so often, maybe he hit his head."

Luke tried to explain. These were Florida bark scorpions. They cost twenty dollars apiece on the Internet. That was Dr. Ford's business—sort of. He sold marine specimens to colleges and laboratories around the country. So why not include live scorpions in his catalog?

"Sell them, plus a few bat houses," Luke reasoned. "And Captain Pony makes the best smoked fish I've ever had. We could help her sell that, too. She wouldn't be poor anymore."

Maribel liked the idea. Sabina did not.

"There's nothing fun about earning money," the girl argued. "Halloween is on Saturday. I'm going to tell Pony that we want to decorate this place and invite her to the marina party. That'll cheer her up."

"She's not going to let us decorate here," Luke countered. "That would attract visitors. And she doesn't like visitors. Remember?"

"She will if I tell her those scorpions are putting wild ideas in your head," Sabina replied tartly.

When Luke protested, "But they're not!" the girl ignored

him. She tossed her pigtails back and started across the lawn to the house.

The old fishing guide was in the back, hoeing a garden that was choked with weeds. There were stalks of corn, and a few pumpkins tucked beneath vines loaded with squash and green tomatoes. Some spiny-looking pineapples planted in a row were golden green and ready to pick.

"Captain Pony, I'm worried about Luke," Sabina began. "He's been working so hard, he claims to see a scorpion under every board he finds. If he doesn't have some fun soon, I'm afraid he'll start seeing even weirder stuff."

The woman leaned against the hoe. She used a bandanna to wipe her face. "Hooray for Luke. Doesn't mean he's weird. Means he's got good eyes."

"You think he's right?"

"Hope so. Scorpions are almost as good as bats when it comes to killing insects. Now, if he found a mess of palmetto bugs in my house, that might bother me. But he won't, 'cause my spiders and scorpions eat them like candy."

Palmetto bugs were what old-time Floridians called great big cockroaches. These roaches could fly and hide in the shadows, where they left piles of poop.

The way the lady's mind worked gave Sabina hope. Bats, scorpions, and spiders fit with the decorations she wanted to make for the Halloween party on Saturday.

Pony, though, refused. No party, she said. And no decorations—not on her property.

The girl felt a chill when the woman pointed in the direction of Bonefield Key. "Besides, I already told you—let the dead spirits rest in peace. You wouldn't like it if folks danced around in costumes and made fun of you. It's the Devil's holiday—that's what some say. I want no part of it. But you kids are still welcome to come here and camp if you want."

Suddenly, Sabina had a different view of Halloween.

"Follow me, young lady," Captain Pony said. She hefted a basket of freshly picked vegetables and started back to the beach. "If you kids want to know how to survive on these islands, you've got a lot more to learn."

When Luke saw Sabina and the old lady coming, he hid the jar of scorpions in his backpack. Maribel pretended not to notice.

Pony placed the vegetables on a picnic table and announced, "When I was a fishing guide, I'd stop at a beach and fix my clients what we called a 'shore lunch.' They loved it because they had to catch or gather their own food and cook over a fire. Wasn't much different for the Calusa and the other settlers who came to Florida hundreds of years ago."

That's how they spent the afternoon. Catching and gathering food for a shore lunch—and learning to cook in the old-fashioned island way.

Something else they learned was how the mound builders had communicated. Captain Pony brought out what she called her "sacred shell horn." She had found it on a Calusa mound when she was a little girl. The seashell was hollow, football-sized, sharp at one end. The other end was wide and knobbed like the crown a king might wear.

On the crown was a pointed spiral. The spiral had been sawed flat to create a blowhole like the mouthpiece of a trumpet. Drilled into the spine of the shell were three perfectly round holes, similar to the holes in a wooden flute.

"The Calusa made this from a horse conch," the woman said, pronouncing the word as "konk." "It's different from most—white as bone and made from a very, very old shell. You can tell from the weight. On quiet nights, you can hear this horn for a mile or more."

To prove it, she slipped her hand inside the shell. She pressed the flat area to her lips. After a deep breath her cheeks puffed out. The sound the shell produced was the mournful wail of a bugle. When her fingers covered the flutelike holes, the tone deepened.

"It might take you a while to get the hang of it," she said, and placed it on the table. The shell was heavy, as if made of marble. The inside spiraled into a series of chambers near the crown.

"Give it a try," Captain Pony said. "You've got to make your lips sort of buzz—and blow hard. Don't worry about playing different notes."

One by one, the kids did.

THIRTEEN
A BEACH LUNCH AND THE MEAN NEIGHBOR

On Captain Pony's property were fruit trees stunted from growing so close to saltwater. Many of the names were strange to Luke. There were knobby golden fruits called guavas. Barbados cherries sort of looked like cherries, but their taste was different. Sea-grape trees grew everywhere— but the same thing. The grapes tasted nothing like grapes back in Ohio. There were also fragrant key limes, and green coconuts littered the ground. Hanging in a larger tree were what the woman called "alligator pears."

In fact, they were huge avocados, three times the size of those sold in stores.

"Gators love to eat avocado pears," she explained. "You

always gotta watch your step when you find a tree near a pond. A gator will grab anything that hits the water—including people, dogs, you name it."

She also warned, "Never eat any fruit or vegetable—even fish—unless you're a hundred percent sure it's safe. It's better to starve than to risk poisoning yourself. A person can live for months on fresh water alone. Forget that nonsense in books about 'edible wild plants.' Too dangerous unless you're an expert—or a fool looking for a trip to the hospital. You kids understand?"

Luke said from experience, "Mushrooms can be really bad news. Cows can die from eating those. And a friend of mine's dog got sick once from eating rhubarb leaves."

Something the boy would've never tried was "prickly pear"—a cactus that grew in sandy areas near the beach. Knives and gloves were required. Lobes of the cactus had to be shaved clean of needles. The same with the rose-colored fruit.

In Cuba, though, prickly pears were a favorite food.

"We love *nopales*," Maribel said, using the Spanish word for the cactus dish. "If you have an onion and a chili pepper, Sabina and I have a good recipe."

"Bird chili peppers grow wild out back. Or help yourselves

to my garden," the woman replied. She was enjoying herself. "First, though, let's catch some fish."

That was easily done off the dock, where the tidal current swirled. There, in a bucket, was a cone of woven nylon—a "cast net," it was called. The mesh was weighted at the bottom with lead balls. At the top was a wrist lanyard spliced to a coil of rope. Years ago, Pony had been one of the best in Florida at "cast-netting" fish.

"My balance isn't good enough now," she admitted. "I get dizzy spells, and I ain't as strong as I used to be. But I can teach you. Who wants to try first?"

The kids took turns. After attaching the wrist lanyard, take a sort of dance step. Swing the net back . . . twist and throw. Do it right, and the net would balloon open like a parachute. The lead weights would then carry the net to the bottom before fish could escape.

Maribel was already good at catching bait for their shark-tagging trips. She went last. With a graceful turn, she spun the net wide and let it sink. When the wrist lanyard began to throb with life, she yanked hard on the rope and pulled the net in hand over hand.

"Heavy," she grunted. "I could use some help."

Luke squatted and lifted with his knees. Dozens of

flopping fish spilled onto the dock. Most had blunt heads and bulging eyes like the headlights of a car.

"Striped mullet," Captain Pony said. "Jumpin' mullet, we call them, because they jump out of the water for no good reason anyone can figure out. You got some beauties there."

"Maybe they jump just to have fun," Sabina suggested.

"Makes as much sense as anything else," the woman said. "Get busy now—grab the smaller fish and put them back in the water while they can still swim away. We don't keep nothing we can't use. That's what I was taught—take care of what lives in the bay. This bay will take care of you."

The kids did as they were told.

It was interesting, listening to the old fishing guide while they prepared their shore lunch. Before refrigeration, she explained, people on the Gulf Coast wouldn't have survived without mullet. The fish could be salted and dried. It was tastier if the splits were cured in a smokehouse at low heat. Female mullet contained sacs of golden eggs—fish roe. The roe could be fried or scrambled into an omelet. In some countries, buyers paid a lot of money for Florida mullet roe.

"That's how a lot of us fisherfolk made our living," Pony said. "What we didn't catch, we grew. Or gathered from trees planted long ago by those skunk-in-the-weeds Spaniards."

The term "skunk-in-the-weeds" had become a private joke. It lightened the mood when they sat down at a table they had moved to the beach. The breeze was better there.

"Looks *fantástico*," Sabina said.

Luke used his beginner's Spanish to agree.

"Hold your horses," the woman said. "This used to be a tradition on this island before folks gave thanks over a fire and ate." She put the ancient shell horn to her lips and blew three joyous notes. It sort of sounded liked like a French horn.

"There now." She grinned. "Dig in."

The table was loaded with food. There was a platter of fried mullet. It was covered with a pepper sauce of cactus, onion, and lime. Potatoes had been buried in the fire. The potato skins had a delicious charcoal taste when served with butter. There was also corn on the cob and a pitcher of iced tea.

Coconut shells became fruit bowls. Coconut water—"milk," some called it—sweetened sliced Barbados cherries. The fruit mix was okay—not bad, Luke said. But it didn't compare to the whole pineapple they roasted over the coals on a stick. It was basted with wild honey until golden brown, then sliced.

Dessert was the best dish by far. Pony provided her specialty—frozen key lime pie made with Eagle Brand condensed milk. The pie was tart and creamy, like frozen sherbet. But better. A lot better.

"Without a refrigerator, canned milk was all we had to cook with—unless there was a cow handy," the woman said. There was a playful grin on her face. The kids had never seen her so happy.

That changed when her neighbor's sleek cabin cruiser came roaring around the point. They recognized the big engines, the yellow hull, and the gleaming chrome tower.

"That fool," Captain Pony muttered. "He doesn't know diddly about the waters around here. Speeds back and forth no matter the time of day. It just goes to prove, you don't need brains to drive a fancy yacht. Just money."

She addressed Maribel, "You ever see that joker when you're out fishing, go the other way. He's the sort of tourist who gets good captains killed."

As she spoke, the cabin cruiser swerved wildly toward a bank of mangroves on the other side of the bay. Water was shallow there. The yellow hull jolted. The outboard motors kicked a rooster tail of mud and created waves that were the boat's wake.

Maribel yelled, "If he keeps going, he's going to hit those pilings you told us about!"

Bones Gate, she meant.

The driver, hidden inside the cabin, realized he'd left the channel. Without slowing, the cabin cruiser heeled to the right in a high-speed turn. It swerved again and rocketed, out of control, toward Captain Pony's dock.

The old fishing guide got to her feet. She flagged her arms in warning. The kids did the same. Seconds before a collision, the cabin cruiser made another swooping turn. It nearly crashed onto the beach where they were standing, then turned again.

Over the sound of the screaming engines, Sabina hollered, "He did that on purpose!"

They were all frozen in shock by how close they'd come to being crushed by a huge speedboat. Worse, the vessel's twisting path had created a gigantic, circular wake—sort of like a whirlpool.

Those waves were now rolling toward them.

Because Sabina and Luke were closest, they rushed to steady the old lady. But not in time. The first wave that crashed ashore flooded the beach. The next wave knocked Pony off her feet. When she fell, she hit her head on the picnic table.

Maribel didn't see it happen. She was sprinting toward the dock. The little green boat had been flooded and was bucking like a horse as waves continued to hammer the shore.

With a sound like a gunshot—*KER-WHACK!*—the mooring ropes snapped. The little boat was slammed against the pilings, then bobbed free into the bay. The girl skidded to a stop at the end of the dock. She hesitated, then jumped into the drifting boat—something no expert captain should ever do.

Maribel landed in water up to her calves. The boat was sinking. A couple of orange life jackets and a wooden oar were already floating away. Jammed beneath a seat was a plastic bailing bucket. She grabbed the bucket and began shoveling water out as fast as she could. When another big wave washed over the side, the girl knew that bailing was useless.

There was only one way to keep the boat afloat. It was risky, but she had no choice. Maribel sloshed her way aft to the little outboard motor. She primed the fuel hose, opened the choke, and gave the starter cord a mighty pull.

Amazingly, the engine started.

Next came the risky part. Most boats had a drainage hole in the rear deck called a scupper. The hole was sealed with a brass plug to keep water from seeping into the hull. If the plug got loose or fell out, the boat would flood.

But the scupper was there for a reason. Maribel had the courage to try what Captain Hannah had taught them to do in an emergency like this. She knelt and felt around blindly. When her fingers found the scupper plug, she yanked it out.

Immediately, water began to boil into the hull. Within a few seconds, the boat would sink.

The race was on.

Maribel plopped down beside the motor. She clanked the engine into gear and twisted the throttle. The little boat tilted dangerously as water sloshed to the back. She twisted the throttle harder and the boat began to gain speed. Slowly, slowly at first, then faster.

The girl glanced down and confirmed that the water was now rushing to escape through the scupper hole. She increased speed and began to steer in wide, smooth circles. This caused the water to drain faster. Soon the boat was skipping across the surface.

When all the hull was drained, Maribel sealed the hole with the brass plug. She slowed to idle speed and recovered the missing life jackets and paddle.

"Hooray for you!" Captain Pony called to her from shore. "Maribel, you are the finest young captain I've seen in many a year. You can use my boat anytime you want. I never told a person that before."

Pleased by the compliment, the girl turned toward the beach and smiled—until she saw that the old fishing guide had been hurt by her fall. The woman was lying on her side, unable to get to her feet.

Luke was kneeling beside her. "She won't let us call an ambulance," he hollered. "Sabina went to phone Doc and Hannah for help. The police should arrest that crock-of-manure."

The sleek cabin cruiser had stopped on its way back to the big concrete house. Maribel could see the driver now. It was the same man who had yelled threats about killing Carlos and feeding the goose to a snake.

The man's broad face pivoted from Pony, who was lying on the sand, to Maribel. He pumped his fist as if celebrating a victory, then sped away.

He was laughing.

FOURTEEN
A WITCH'S MASK AND HEAVY FOG

On Thursday afternoon they visited Pony in the hospital. She had hurt her head and would be there for a couple of days.

"Would it be okay if the kids stayed at my place over the weekend?" the woman asked Hannah, who had driven them in her SUV. "Doctor says I should be on my feet again after they take more X-rays and such. My chickens and livestock need lookin' after."

Hannah agreed they would all help.

On Friday morning, the wind changed. The temperature dropped. By late afternoon, the warm water of Dinkins Bay was covered with a drifting silver mist.

Doc summoned the kids to his lab. "I know you plan on camping tonight," he said, "but you can't take a rental boat. Too dangerous. The forecast calls for heavy fog. So why not just stay home? If the fog lifts, you can camp out tomorrow night."

"But Pony's counting on us," Sabina protested. "We've already got our tent set up and everything. Who's going to feed the chickens in the morning and her stupid goose if we're not there?"

Luke, who seldom complained, reminded the biologist, "The marina's Halloween party is tomorrow and we have school on Monday. That would only give us one night. And her house is close to here even without a boat."

The biologist cared about the old fishing guide. That was obvious.

"You win," he said, smiling. "Throw your bikes and gear in the back of my truck. I'll drive you to Pony's place now. If you have any kind of trouble, you can ride your bikes home. Or I can be there in ten minutes."

The animals had been fed. Carlos, the goose, had been herded into her pen—after chasing Sabina around the yard and snapping at her backside. Even Maribel had laughed because Sabina was wearing the black hooded robe and witch's mask she'd bought for Halloween. The mask was horrid—with warts and fangs, and skin like rubbery green cheese.

It was a ridiculous sight to see.

"I hate that goose," the girl complained. By then she'd stored the mask in her backpack. "I don't know who is worse—Carlos, or Pony's skunk-in-the-weeds neighbor. The police should have arrested that mean man."

"He told them it never happened," Maribel reminded her sister. "We didn't have proof."

"The guy lied," Luke said. "He tried to sink Pony's boat on purpose. Next time, we should take video."

The sun had just set. They sat by a smudge fire on the beach in front of Pony's house. Nearby was a blue tent shaped like a mushroom. Hannah had helped them set it up yesterday after their visit to the hospital. Doc had loaned Luke what he called a "jungle hammock." The hammock was strung between two coconut palms beneath a tunnel of bug netting.

The biologist had just pulled away in his truck. The kids

liked Doc, but it was nice to finally be alone in this private spot on the bay. The fire popped and crackled. Sparks soared toward a cloud that drifted, shadowlike, across the bay.

"That's a fog bank coming, I think," Maribel said. "Just like Doc predicted. We should cook dinner while we can still see without flashlights. The moon won't be up until late. And we need to store dry clothes and blankets and stuff in the tent because of the fog. It'll soak everything like rain."

They had already buried three sweet potatoes in the fire. On the picnic table were vegetables from the garden. Luke sliced yellow squash and a couple of green tomatoes into an iron skillet. Sabina insisted on adding a chili pepper, and chunks of cactus and onions. A container of brown rice, already cooked, had been brought from home.

"Tomorrow morning we'll have time to catch some fish," the boy said, placing the skillet on the fire. "Or we can wade around and find a clam bed. I've never eaten steamed clams. That might be good. Or oysters. Pony said it's best to collect oysters at low tide."

"Just vegetables and rice are enough for me—as long as it's spicy," Sabina responded. She swatted a mosquito near her eye. A moment later, she jumped up and sputtered a string of words in Spanish.

Luke grinned. His Spanish was improving.

"Stop swearing," Maribel warned. "What's wrong?"

"Ay-ay-ay!" the girl responded. She was walking in circles, still wearing her hooded witch's robe. "My eye burns like it's on fire."

"Because of those little red bird peppers you picked," Luke told her. "You didn't wash your hands after cutting them up." He got to his feet. "Let's go inside the house. Maybe Pony has some milk in the fridge."

"Stop laughing, farm boy," Sabina said. "I'm not thirsty. My eye's on fire."

Luke shared what he'd been taught in gardening class: milk was better than water when it came to treating the sting of a chili pepper. "If there's no milk," he added, "you need to wash your eye out in the sink. Especially after handling bird peppers. Man, those little stinkers are hot."

"You and that stupid 4-H club," the girl responded. "Like you know everything. Get out of my way."

She trotted across the yard into the house.

Maribel was right about the cloud drifting toward them. It was a wall of fog. The last orange streaks of sunset vanished behind a dripping haze that swept across the beach. The temperature dropped.

From where Luke sat, he could see Pony's dock and little boat. They disappeared, too, when the wind died. Fog settled around them in the darkness and formed a silver dome over the campfire. It was like being inside a cave.

From the direction of the house, Sabina called, "Where'd everybody go? Are you still there?" She'd been gone for several minutes.

A flashlight stabbed the darkness. Like a Jedi sword, a white beam attempted to hack its way through the mist. The flashlight blinked off. Muttering, the girl stepped into the circle created by the fire. She took a seat between Maribel and Luke.

"I've never seen fog this thick," she said. "A flashlight just makes it worse. I'd hate to be out in a boat on a night like this. Doc was right."

In her hand was an old hardback book.

"Look what I found. It's the book Pony told us about." She flipped through a few pages. "Here's a drawing of the gold medallion. And a bunch of other stuff made by the Calusa people."

Maribel frowned. "You didn't go snooping through her house, did you?"

"Just a few drawers and shelves," the girl replied. She had

opened the book. "We were told to make ourselves at home. I found some other interesting stuff, too."

"Like what?"

"Wait until Pony gets back," the girl replied. "I'll show you then—if Pony gives me permission."

They scooted their chairs closer to the fire. The skillet bubbled on a bed of coals. Wood smoke was scented by the simmering stew of onions, vegetables, and rice.

Maribel passed the book to Luke. "Here it is," she said, referring to a strange drawing that filled half a page.

The boy wasn't sure what a medallion was. To him the object looked more like a small wood carving. It was shaped sort of like the head of an alligator.

"Or a crocodile," Sabina suggested. "Don't those look like fangs?"

"More like teardrops," Maribel said. "Those little square holes could be eyes. Isn't there a saying about crocodile tears?"

Luke had never heard of that before. Above what might be a crocodile's eyes were circles within a circle. At first he thought of a target at a gun range. Then he had another idea. "When the moon is full, I've seen circles around it sort of like that." He glanced up at a smear of gray that might have been the moon. Or was it reflected light from the fire? "Doc told me the circles were caused by ice crystals way up in the sky."

There were other drawings and photos in the book— including one of a seashell horn that looked a lot like the one Captain Pony had found. It was large, bone white, with knobs like a crown.

This gave them something to talk about while they ate. The stew and the sweet potatoes, topped with fresh butter, were delicious. For dessert, they skinned another pineapple and roasted it on a stick.

After the dishes were done, wood was added to the fire. The kids kept their voices low. Fog magnified every small sound. In the mangroves, sleepy birds squabbled. The distant strumming of a guitar reached them from the marina. A tinkle of laughter floated across the bay, then vanished in mist.

Sabina and Maribel wondered if it was their mother having fun. Suddenly the girls felt lonely. The marina was so close, yet their home seemed as distant as the invisible stars above.

They stayed up late. Maribel phoned Hannah with a final check-in. Luke was the last to go to bed. He climbed into the jungle hammock and zipped the netting closed. His hearing, which was always good, became radar-like in the midnight silence. Water dripped. Slow waves washed the beach as if the bay were breathing.

The boy drifted off to sleep. Hours later, he was jolted awake by the clatter of a small boat starting. Eyes open, ears alert, he tracked the boat to an area near Bonefield Key.

The engine went off. Several minutes passed. The noises Pony had warned them about began. He heard what might have been the cries of a baby animal. Then grunts and groans, and the faint howling of a dog.

To the boy, the noises sounded fake, as if played through a speaker.

Next came the screech of a shovel striking seashells. It

went on for a while. Not loud. But loud enough to alert Carlos. The goose responded with angry honks and whistles.

Luke pulled his pants on and grabbed his backpack. He swung out of the hammock and laced his boots. Overhead, the moon broke through a hole in the fog. The sky was on fire with blue light.

Sabina and Maribel were standing outside their tent, fully dressed. Each girl had a blanket around her shoulders. The noises had awoken them, too.

"I bet it's that skunk-in-the-weeds neighbor," Sabina whispered. "Could be he's at the Bone Tunnel digging up Periwinkle's grave—and I know why. He's looking for the gold medallion. We've got to stop him."

"Bonefield Key," Maribel corrected in a whisper. "We can't. It's five thirty in the morning. Too early to call Doc or Hannah. Besides, we don't have a boat."

"Yes, we do," her sister argued. "Pony said you could use her boat anytime. We all heard her. This time we'll take the video camera and get evidence. Unless you're scared."

"I'm just trying to follow the rules," Maribel replied. She turned to Luke for his opinion.

"Nothing to be scared of," Luke said. "Those animal

noises are bogus, I'm pretty sure. In Ohio, hunters use these little electronic gadgets called game callers. Like amplifiers in a waterproof can. The hunters operate the sounds from their phones—all kinds of animal calls. I think the guy's just trying to upset Pony. He doesn't know she's not here."

Before they could discuss it, the goose came charging through the fog. Carlos had escaped from her pen. Honking, the angry bird flapped off in the direction of Bonefield Key. She disappeared into the fog.

"Oh no!" Sabina gasped. "The man will kill Carlos if she bites him again. We've got no choice now. We've got to follow her."

For Maribel, it was not an easy decision. But when the goose's distant honks became a series of panicked squawks, she panicked, too. "Okay. Everyone get your life jackets on. Grab your backpacks, too—and make sure you have a flashlight. Luke, do you have the first-aid kit?

Luke shouldered his bag. "A whole survival kit. I'll get the boat ready."

FIFTEEN
CROCODILE POACHERS ESCAPE

The motor on Pony's boat was too loud, so they used the oars to row in what they hoped was the direction of Bonefield Key. Fog swirled. It was impossible to see more than a few feet in any direction. Behind them, the light of their campfire disappeared after only a few strokes.

Maribel had a terrible feeling in her stomach. It was like being a thousand feet up in the sky, floating through a cloud in an airplane. She gave up gave up and let the boat drift.

"I have no idea where we are," she whispered. "I'm not even sure how to get back to our camp. This is dangerous."

The echoing growl of a crocodile startled them all. It seemed to come from the left, not far away. The goose added a few pathetic squawks.

"Over there," Luke said. He had his hands cupped to his eyes. "I see lights. You don't hear voices?"

Sabina was bundled up in her witch's cloak. She pushed the hood aside. It was irritating that the boy could see and hear what she couldn't. "I think I do," she lied. "Which way? I'm worried about that stupid goose."

The boy pointed.

Maribel turned the boat slightly and resumed rowing quietly. She was careful not to bang the oars or let them slap the water.

Through the fog, a circle of dark poles appeared. They might have been an ancient temple. Maribel held her breath until she remembered that an old shack had once been here.

Bones Gate, the locals had named the circle of dangerous pilings.

A black ledge emerged. It was a mangrove shoreline. After a few cautious strokes, Maribel allowed the boat to glide in silence. Tidal current pushed them toward an object that loomed ahead. It was tall, curved like the neck of a dinosaur.

"A dead tree," Luke whispered. He got up, his stance wide, ready for a jolt. Their little boat crunched onto shallow oyster shells. He got an arm around the tree. The boat swung sideways into an opening.

"Now do you see the light?" he asked, barely moving his lips.

Yes, they did. An underwater spotlight illuminated a circle of water that boiled with fog. It took a moment before Maribel recognized where they were. It was same little pond where they had seen the crocodile days before. The oranges and the shell mound they had found were on the opposite side of this tiny island.

A strangely shaped boat appeared from the mist. It was flat and long. On the console glowed the screen of an electronic GPS chart. The silhouette of a man stood on the stern. He steered by using a long pole. He was huge, broad-shouldered—probably Pony's neighbor. Another shadow person controlled the bright underwater spotlight. The light created a circle of green that probed ahead of the strange boat.

The neighbor's gruff voice demanded, "Where'd the freakin' thing go? Turn the game caller on again. Volume loud this time."

"Don't rush me," the other man said. "I can only do one thing at a time, Leon."

Leon. That had to be the name of Pony's new neighbor.

Luke had been right about the bogus noises. There was a

sudden electronic *whuff* of a crocodile, then a rumbling growl. Next came the tweeting *gunk-gulp-purr* cries of baby crocs.

The recordings were played over and over. After a short silence, the men received a thunderous response that was lionlike.

It was the real crocodile. And the crocodile was very, very close.

"Here she comes. See the size of that monster?" Leon said. He sounded excited. "Good! She's carrying a bunch of babies on her back. Steady now, steady. I'll get ready with the cast net."

The man knelt to lift a cast net off the deck. He cursed when he nearly lost his balance. "Donny, you dimwit," Leon said to his partner. "Don't screw this up. Keep that stupid light underwater or you'll blind us both in this fog."

It was true. The beam of a bright light turned the swirling cloud into a mirror. It was impossible to see anything.

"Sorry, boss," the skinny man, Donny, said. The spotlight angled downward. From the shadows, a huge, dark shape cruised into the circle of green water. Only the crocodile's head broke the surface. Clustered on the croc's back were five or six babies. The tails of two other infants stuck out from the creature's teeth like whiskers. There was no way of knowing how many more hatchlings were hiding nearby.

The kids watched from the shadows as Leon looped the cast net over his shoulder and prepared to throw it.

Sabina leaned closer to Luke. "He's evil," she whispered. "He wants to kill the mother or steal those babies. Probably sell them for a lot of money on the Internet just like Doc told us. What happened to Carlos?"

Maribel interrupted by speaking into her sister's ear. "Not another word. *Please.* I've got the video camera ready. We need evidence. Just sit quietly and see what happens."

Luke pressed a finger to his lips in agreement. He had noticed a plastic garbage bag on the deck of the flat, wide boat. Something inside the bag was silent but moving as if very angry. It was Carlos, he guessed. The men had caught the goose. They had probably taped the bird's beak and legs to keep it from getting away.

Maribel saw what happened next through the camera's viewfinder.

The crocodile seemed unaware of the strange-looking boat—until the big man stomped his foot. That changed everything. Frightened, the giant reptile sank with a splash.

Leon twisted and threw the net as the babies went skittering across the surface.

Too late. The net opened like a large spiderweb. Lead weights crashed the surface and dragged the infants to the bottom.

Sabina allowed a horrified groan to escape her lips. Puzzled, Leon glanced in their direction as he towed the net in. Tangled in the net were six or seven crocodile babies. Their chirping no longer sounded like little birds. They grunted rapid-fire, terrified.

"Hurry up," Leon ordered. "Get that box open and throw them in there. Watch your fingers!"

"Yes, sir, boss," Donny replied.

Maribel continued to shoot video. The men went to work until they heard a whuffing growl. Concerned, they turned to look. In the pool of green light, the giant reptile had surfaced. Its body was puffed up wide, scales shiny beneath the swirling fog. The animal's pointed snout made another whuffing sound. A massive tail slapped the water, and the creature rocketed toward the boat.

Leon realized they were being attacked. He lunged, got the engine started, and swung the boat around. The motor's propeller kicked a muddy stream into the shallows. Close behind was the mother crocodile. In a panic, Leon opened the throttle. It was a race, but the creature wasn't fast enough. The strange-looking boat zoomed past within a few feet of the kids. It was a tense moment, but the spotlight's glare and the fog protected them from being seen.

The mother crocodile drifted to a stop. She made a pathetic grunting noise and waited on the surface. Only two of her snakelike babies reappeared. The animal opened its jaws. The babies scurried in. They all sank to the bottom.

Sabina didn't realize she was crying. "We've got to get back to the house and call Hannah or Doc. Do you think they killed Carlos?"

When Luke was angry (which was rare), his voice softened because he was prone to stutter. *You stutter 'cause you've got no confidence, and you never will,* his stepfather in Ohio had chided the boy more than once. There was nothing wrong with stuttering. A lot of people stuttered. But Luke didn't stutter now. "Carlos is okay. The goose is in that garbage bag. Let's go."

"In this fog?" Maribel asked. "Where? I don't know how to get back to our camp."

"They've got an electronic chart and a GPS," the boy replied. "It'll lead them back to the guy's dock. So just follow their wake until we get near Pony's place."

Maribel patted her pocket to confirm the camera was safe. "Good idea. The sun will be up in an hour or so. Hopefully, the video came out. We'll show Doc and Hannah."

"We don't have time," Sabina insisted. Furious, she slammed her little backpack on the deck. "We've got to sneak down to that ugly house before the man kills Carlos."

Luke had been thinking the same thing. "Yeah. And maybe rescue those baby crocodiles if we get a chance."

SIXTEEN

TRAPPED BY THIEVES AND A RATTLESNAKE

The lights on the new neighbor's dock were smoky yellow in the fog. The kids arrived on foot in time to watch the two men load the box of baby crocodiles onto the sleek cabin cruiser. It was one of several boxes they carried from a storage shed to the boat.

Next, the heavy garbage bag was thrown aboard. It landed with a fleshy thud. Leon, the biggest of the two, swung the bag into the cabin, down what sounded like stairs.

"The goose is still alive," Luke whispered. "I could see the bag moving."

Maribel had to grab her sister's arm. "Don't lose your temper. Wait and let's see what they do."

When the men clumped, heavy-footed, across the yard to the house, Maribel shouldered her backpack and crept closer. Luke and Sabina followed. Fog made it impossible to see much but the dock and moonlight reflecting off the windows of the huge concrete house.

A hedge of mangroves made a good place to hide. They squatted there, still wearing the inflatable suspender-like life vests. A door slammed. Lights flickered on inside the house. At least one of the men had gone upstairs to the second floor.

"Think they're coming back?" Luke asked.

Maribel replied, "I wonder what's in those other boxes. Maybe Sabina was right—they catch baby crocodiles and other animals and sell them. That's illegal. We should go back to Pony's place and call the police."

"Carlos will be dead by then," Sabina insisted. "She'll suffocate in that bag."

Luke got up. "I'll go get her. If those guys come out of the house, whistle or something to warn me."

"No," Maribel said. Her heart pounded as she pictured what might happen. "We can't separate. That's a team rule. We all go. If they catch us, we'll—"

"They're not going to catch us," Sabina said. She grabbed

her little backpack and trotted off into the fog. Luke and Maribel scampered after her.

It was a long dock with railings. The odd little boat the men had used was tiny compared to the craft at the end of the dock. The cabin cruiser was two stories high with a tower. Its powerful motors had been tilted down. Tied above the motors was a tiny inflatable boat with oars—a dinghy. Maybe the men were preparing for a long trip.

One by one, the kids climbed over the cruiser's railing and crawled across the deck to the cabin door. Maribel went last. "When you get inside," she whispered, "don't turn on any lights. Use a flashlight."

Sabina replied sharply in Spanish. She was frustrated. Her light was buried in her bag beneath a diary, the green witch's mask, and a bunch of other stuff.

"I've got mine," Luke said. "I'll go first."

He opened the door and stepped into a dark space that smelled of plastic and cigar smoke. "Maybe you two should stand guard out here. I won't be long."

"Move your butt, pig farmer," Sabina ordered in Spanish.

Luke had heard the phrase so many times, he understood. He switched on his light. The cabin was equipped like a deluxe RV. Beneath a bank of windows were plush captain's chairs. The console was loaded with electronic screens, all dark. But there were no boxes or a garbage bag.

To the right was a wooden stairway. Sabina followed the boy down to a lower deck. There were storage closets along the wall. At the front of the boat, behind a curtain, was an oversized bed beneath a pair of porthole windows. Orange life jackets were piled there. They were the big puffy kind that were uncomfortable to wear. Stacked on the floor outside the curtain were several plastic boxes with lids. The garbage bag lay nearby.

Sabina rushed and tore the bag open. There was Carlos. The goose's orange eyes blinked at the brightness of the flashlight. The men had used electrical tape on the bird's beak and legs. Sabina cradled the goose in her arms and made cooing noises. Carlos struggled briefly, then seemed to understand.

"Don't take the tape off yet," Luke whispered. "She'll start honking. The way sound travels in fog, they'll hear."

Maribel was at the top of the stairs keeping watch. "What about the baby crocs?" she called down. There was a sense of urgency in her voice.

"Are the men coming?" Luke asked.

"I'm not sure. I might have heard a door close, but I can't

see the house because of the fog. Did you find the babies yet?"

Luke squatted by the plastic containers. There were six. The lids were heavy plastic, pocked with airholes. He couldn't see inside, so he opened the lid of the nearest.

"Turtles," he whispered. "A bunch of them. Newly hatched, I think. They don't look like sea turtles."

Sabina was stroking the goose's back. She glanced down at a scrambling mass of small turtles. Their round, leathery-looking shells were caramel brown.

"Hurry up," Maribel called. "Check the other boxes."

Luke popped three more lids. They all contained dozens of small turtles. But a different type. Many had hard shells splotched with diamond shapes.

In the next box were the baby crocodiles. Seven of them. In the flashlight's glare, their eyes sparked with red as if a fire burned inside. Their high-pitched *gunk-gulp-purr* chirping vibrated through the boat's fiberglass hull.

"Quiet," Sabina hissed. "You want those bad men to hear you?"

Luke pulled the last box closer and popped the latches. Inside was a mound of wood shavings covered by a towel. The boy was about to pull the towel away when he heard a familiar noise. It was the sound of sizzling grease. His hand froze, inches away.

The sizzling sound stopped. The towel moved. Something curled beneath it. The towel mushroomed upward into the shape of a coiled snake.

At the same instant, Maribel came flying down the steps. "They're coming," she said. "I didn't see them until too late. We've got to hide."

Luke fumbled the lid when he tried to reseal the container. It went clattering onto the deck as Maribel grabbed her sister's arm.

"Hurry," she whispered. "Get behind the curtain. And turn out that light!"

The last thing the boy saw before the room went dark was a snake sliding over the rim of the box. Its body was long and thick. Its scales were decorated with bars of cinnamon and gold.

Leon and his partner had captured the rattlesnake that Luke had almost stepped on. It was free now.

But where?

"Get on the bed," Luke urged the girls. Maribel had already pulled the curtain closed. "Don't let your legs dangle over the side. I mean it."

They hadn't seen the snake, but they heard the fear in the boy's voice.

The cabin cruiser tilted with the weight of the men when they stepped aboard. Leon's harsh voice was low and distinctive.

"Donny—get away from that fridge. You've had enough beer for one night. Go below and make sure those boxes are sealed tight."

His partner's nervous laughter was like ice clinking in a glass. "No need, boss. Already checked them. Why don't we both have another beer? This fog gives me the creeps."

"Creeps? You're scared of a little fog?"

Donny sounded scared when he replied, "Dude, it's Halloween. Could be anything out there. Ghosts from that grave you started to dig up. Werewolves, the walking dead. Who knows on a night like this?"

Sabina smiled at what she'd just heard.

Leon had an ugly laugh. "Werewolves my butt. You've got the brains of a ten-year-old. You know that?"

"Seriously, boss. Strange things happen on foggy nights. I saw this TV show—a documentary with experts. The thing was on the Internet, so it had to be true. I've studied this stuff."

"Uh-huh. Stop arguing and do what I say. Go below, and don't mess with that garbage bag. If that crazy goose isn't dead, it will be soon."

"Snake food," Donny said with sarcasm. "Perfect. Animal sacrifices on Halloween. Sounds like something a zombie would do. I saw this zombie movie once. And, boss, it was so freakin' real—"

Leon hollered, "Shut your mouth and do what you're told."

Muttering, the skinny man came down the stairs and hit a light switch. Luke scooted away from the curtain. The sisters were on the other side of the bed, huddled among the big, puffy life jackets. The goose, its beak and legs taped, was wedged between them.

The rattlesnake had disappeared.

Maribel looked at Luke. She touched a finger to her lips. Sabina was whispering a prayer or a magic spell while she tugged at her blue-and-yellow cowrie necklace. Behind the girls, a porthole showed a wisp of fog in the moonlight. The sound of a fast, outgoing tide could be heard through the fiberglass hull.

Footsteps approached the bed. The curtain rustled. The

man was either drunk or scared—or both. He didn't take time to notice the empty garbage bag or the open box.

"Dude doesn't believe anything I say," Donny grumbled. He returned up the stairs in a hurry.

The light went out.

Leon's gruff voice hollered orders. "Check the running lights. Untie those ropes from the dock. Do I have to tell you everything? No—don't come back into the cabin. I want you up front to keep watch. We're leaving."

"Stand outside, you mean?" Donny complained. "No way, boss. This fog is freaking me out, man. The sun will be up soon. Why not wait? Neither one of us knows much about this boating stuff. You said so yourself."

Leon's response was loud and profane.

"Have another beer if it'll shut that yap of yours," the man added. "Stand at the front railing—that's an order. With all these computer screens, this boat practically drives itself. Even you could do it. You might see something up there that I don't."

"Then why don't we trade off?" Donny hollered back. "Please, boss. *Please.* You drive first, then we'll trade places. Think about it, huh?"

Leon found his partner's pleading tone infuriating. "You're making me crazy. Know that? Sure . . . I'll get us into deep water, then you can drive—until I change my mind. Which won't take long."

That got a booming laugh out of the big man.

Four huge outboard motors rumbled to life. The sleek cabin cruiser banged the dock hard and pulled away.

The kids were trapped.

SEVENTEEN
A BOAT CRASH AT BONES GATE

Maribel didn't panic until she felt the cabin cruiser go faster and reach top speed. She got on her knees and looked through the porthole window. All she saw was a spotlight's beam and mist rocketing toward them.

Maribel was an experienced boater. If she couldn't see, it meant the driver couldn't see. At any second, they could crash into the mangroves or hit a dock. She also knew the tide was flowing from the bay into the Gulf of Mexico. There were a lot of shallow oyster bars and rocks in the area.

By then the boat was lunging across the water like a greyhound.

"That man's a fool," she said over the roar of the engines.

"He's using a spotlight. That's the dumbest thing you can do in heavy fog. We've got to stop him before he kills someone—maybe us."

Sabina was scared and mad. "He's drunk. They're both drunk. I hate them." The cruiser slammed through another wave. The girl had to cling to the goose to keep them from being thrown off the bed.

"We've got to do something," Luke said. "But I can't get to the engines. They'll see me. And we're going too fast to jump overboard."

When Maribel took out a small flashlight, he stopped her. "We don't need that. You'll blind me. There's plenty of light coming through the porthole for me to see."

He didn't want to startle the rattlesnake.

"Our eyes aren't as good as yours," the girl reminded him. "There has to be a hatch down here that opens into the bottom hull. We might be able to cut the fuel hose. Or find the fuse box and kill the boat's electrical system. That would stop them." She snapped her fingers. "Or pull the drain plugs out—like I did to save Pony's boat. If they slow down for some reason, the boat will flood."

Luke had to picture it in his mind. Even expensive cabin cruisers had a drainage area at the rear called a bilge. He'd spent enough time working at the marina to know. Inside the bilge would be all sorts of stuff—fuel hoses, electric wires, and pumps.

He nodded. "Yeah, that's smart. I'll go. It's safer. I won't need a flashlight to see."

Sabina interrupted, "I've got a better idea."

"What?"

"This." She reached into her backpack and found what she wanted by feel. It was her horrid witch's mask with the warts and green rubber skin. "I'll sneak up there and scare them so bad, they'll both jump overboard. Then we'll steal their boat and call for help on the radio. I already put a hex on those two. They'll be sorry!"

When the girl was angry, she often claimed to use magic spells and curses to get her way.

"Scare two grown men?" Luke said. He might have laughed if he didn't believe the girl had some sort of weird, witchy powers. "I don't know . . . Let's try Maribel's plan first. Wait here and I'll try to find the bilge. Or the electrical switches."

"Sabina can stay," Maribel said. She braced herself when the boat slammed through another wave. "Someone has to look after Carlos. But I'm coming with you."

Luke slid under the curtain, saying, "Just give me one minute out there alone. Okay?"

"Who's he whispering to?" Sabina wondered. "Those boxes full of turtles? If the turtles are smart, they'll ignore him."

The girls could hear bits and pieces of Luke saying in a soothing tone, "I'm not going to hurt you. Hey . . . remember me? Why not come out and let me see where you are?"

It was the voice he used when calming an aggressive dog.

The engines were loud. There was wind noise, too. The boat had to be going forty miles per hour.

"This is insane," Maribel said to her sister. "We've got to get out of here before we crash. Stay here with the goose unless I call you."

Maribel slipped through the curtain.

Sabina waited until the curtain was closed to say, "I still like my idea better."

The girl touched her beaded necklace and closed her eyes. She resumed chanting words she had learned in Cuba from the magic women.

Luke didn't hear Maribel tiptoe up behind him. He jumped when he felt her hand touch his arm, then took a long, deep breath to calm himself.

"Holy moly, you scared the fire out of me."

"Find it yet?" Maribel whispered. It was hard to keep her balance because the cruiser was slamming waves at high speed.

For a dopey moment, the boy thought she was asking about the snake. "No, but it has to be around here somewhere. Hiding in some dark place, probably, all curled up to stay warm. I wouldn't worry about it."

In the dim light, Maribel squinted at him. "I meant the hatch to the bilge area. Hatches can't hide. And they don't curl up to stay warm. Who were you talking to just now?"

"Myself," the boy said. "People do it all the time." It was a rare lie, but the situation was bad enough without involving a rattlesnake.

Maribel glanced at the steps to the upper deck. Light filtered down. Loud music had been added to the noise of the huge outboard motors. Leon and Donny were up there. One was at the steering wheel. The other was probably outside on the front of the cruiser keeping watch. No telling if the men had switched places.

"I brought my flashlight," Maribel said, "and I'm going to use it. Not all of us can see in the dark like an owl. Come on."

She moved past the boy to the back of the boat. She knelt, felt around with her hands, and switched on the light. It revealed a hatch built into the floor.

"This could be it," she said. "Help me get it open. We might need this." Maribel unfolded the multi-tool holstered on her belt. She used the pliers for leverage on a steel latch. The fiberglass door tilted open.

"*Yes!*" Luke exclaimed. "Shine the light."

The bilge area was doormat-sized, sunk into the hull. Dirty water covered the drainage scuppers. Bolted to the transom were bilge pumps, hoses, wires, and four metal cans that were fuel filters. Attached to each filter was a hose and a brass valve.

"This boat has four motors," Luke reasoned. "A fuel filter for each. I'm not sure, but those valves might control the fuel."

"Cut the hoses, you think?" Maribel had already opened the knife blade.

Luke stared at the colorful electrical wires—red, yellow, green, blue. He was familiar with red and green wires. Same as on the farm tractor he'd fixed many times. The wires could produce sparks. Cut a gas hose, the boat might explode.

"Try closing those brass valves first," he suggested. "You'll need the pliers again. If they're part of the fuel line, it might take a few minutes, but those big outboards will go dry fast. When the boat stops, we can grab the baby crocs and jump."

Maribel didn't like the idea of jumping overboard. They had practiced a similar emergency with Hannah a few days ago. Even though they all wore inflatable vests, it was risky. "We have to take Carlos, too," she reminded the boy. "Then call the police when we get ashore."

The kids went to work. Maribel twisted two of the valves closed. Luke helped wrestle the third valve, which was stuck. They were so busy, they didn't notice Sabina peeking through the curtains. She had freed the goose's legs but left its beak taped as a precaution.

It didn't matter. Maribel had the pliers on the fourth valve when several bad things happened at once. The fiberglass hull jolted—a terrible grinding sound. The cruiser tilted as if about to flip over. Powerful engines shrieked during a turn that hurled the kids across the deck on their bellies. Luke collided with the stack of plastic boxes. The boxes went flying.

From above came a man's wild scream. The man's scream faded like the whistle of a passing train.

The boat picked up speed, then crashed hard into something with a jarring explosion. There was a sound of fiberglass colliding with solid wood.

Once again, the kids went skittering across the deck. For a moment they lay on their bellies in dazed silence. Maribel couldn't figure out what had happened—until she saw water flooding in through the side of the boat. The fiberglass hull had been ripped open by something.

From above, Donny's voice shouted, "Leon! Where are you? Answer me, Leon. Hang on, I'll throw you a life jacket—if I can find one."

The skinny man came clumping down the stairs. He was in such a panic he didn't notice Maribel and Luke crouching in darkness, up to their knees in water. He switched on a flashlight and threw open the curtains—then stumbled back in terror at what he saw.

Sabina had put on her horrid green witch's mask. And Carlos was free. The goose pecked the man hard on the forehead. At the same instant, the girl raised her hands as if they were claws and shrieked, "BOO! BOO! BOO! I put a hex on you!"

Donny made a yipping sound. He turned and sprinted up the stairs, crying, "Stay away . . . stay away . . . leave me alone."

Carlos went after the man in a rage. Sabina followed, cackling like a witch in the movies. A moment later, they heard a heavy splash. Donny had jumped overboard. A softer splash meant the goose was in the water, too.

Maribel got to her feet. "Luke, grab the box with the baby crocodiles. I've got to find Sabina, then radio the Coast Guard for help. We can save the turtles later."

The girl hurried topside while Luke struggled with the box. It was too large to carry under one arm. So he dumped the baby crocs into the garbage bag. When he did, he heard the familiar sound of sizzling grease.

This time, he did need a flashlight. Yes . . . the snake had already crawled into the garbage bag. With no time to worry, he knotted the bag and held it away from his legs. As he carried it up the steps, the baby crocodiles resumed their frantic chirping, and the snake's sizzling calmed.

"The radio doesn't work," Maribel shouted. She and Sabina were standing at the steering wheel. "Nothing works. Not even the lights. We've got to help save those men, then figure a way to get ashore. Grab your backpacks and inflate your life vests. This boat is sinking!"

One by one, the kids pulled the emergency tabs on their vests, which ballooned around their necks like thick rubber suspenders.

The cabin windows showed a misty slash of silver to the east. Protruding from the fog were seven dark pilings that had crushed the boat's hull.

It was sunrise at Bones Gate on Halloween morning.

EIGHTEEN
NO HONOR AMONG THIEVES

Donny was somewhere out there in the fog, begging the goose, "Stop it, you freakin' duck! Stay away!" and then calling Leon's name. Over and over, he hollered, "Boss, where are you? You okay, Leon?"

The man was terrified.

Finally, Leon answered, "I'm hanging on to one of the posts you hit, you drunken nitwit. I was a fool to let you drive." He cursed and said something about being thrown out of the boat. "Hurt my freakin' shoulder," he groaned. "I'm gonna need help getting back on the boat."

A misty gray ball ballooned above dark trees. It was the sun. Yet the fog was too thick to see more than a few yards in any direction.

Maribel ducked out the cabin door. The sound of men arguing drew her toward the front of the boat. One of the pilings had pierced the hull like a sword. Below, in the water, clinging to the pilings, were Leon and his partner.

She gave Sabina a push toward the stairs. "Go below and grab all the life jackets you can carry. I'll find some rope. We need to rig the jackets like throwing buoys. That'll save them until help arrives."

Luke, still carrying the garbage bag, had followed them outside. Maribel turned to the boy. "That little rubber boat hanging over the motors? Cut it free. Or there should be a crank of some type. Either way, get it into the water—and don't make any sound."

"The dinghy?" he asked to confirm the order. Sabina was already rushing down the stairs. "We can't let those crocks-of-horse-manure take it. We need a boat to get back to Captain Pony's house and call for help."

"I know," Maribel snapped. "Hurry up. Tie the dinghy so it doesn't drift away. Once Sabina and I throw those men life jackets, we're out of here!"

She started to wave the boy away, then paused, her eyes on the garbage bag. The piercing chirps of the baby crocodiles vibrated through the silence of the fog.

"Put the bag in the dinghy, too. We'll release them later."

Luke wasn't crazy about rowing ashore with a bag of baby crocs and a rattlesnake, but now was not the time to argue.

The cabin cruiser was wedged against the pilings as if it had plowed up a ski ramp. He grabbed a handrail and started downhill to the back of the boat and nearly collided with Sabina. Her arms were loaded with bulky orange life jackets, several still wrapped in plastic.

"We can't leave without Carlos," she hollered, as if the bird were Luke's responsibility. "That stupid goose bit me again. You find her, farm boy!"

Luke hurried away without comment. The rubber dinghy hung on poles called a davit. A metal lever allowed the dinghy to swing over the water. The baby crocodiles were chirping loudly and trying to claw their way through the plastic. The snake was slithering around, trying to escape, too.

The temptation was to empty the bag overboard. Instead Luke tossed it into the rubber boat as ordered, and placed his backpack on the deck. This allowed him to concentrate on the davit. There was a crank locked into a series of gears. The gears controlled ropes that could raise or lower the little boat.

But the locking lever was stuck. The boy used both thumbs to try to force the lever open. It wouldn't budge. His pocketknife was too small, so he opened his backpack and found a sheath knife he'd bought for 4-H camping trips. The handle was solid steel.

The boy was hammering away at the lever when Maribel screamed from the front of the boat, "Stop! Stop!"

Immediately, Luke did—until he realized she was yelling to Leon and his partner.

"Let go of that rope," Maribel demanded, grunting as if struggling with something heavy. "I mean it—stop! You're going to pull my sister into the water. We're trying to help you!"

The boy froze, his radar ears alert. He heard Sabina scream a familiar curse word in Spanish. Next there was a sickening thud, followed by a splash.

The blue lightning eye within Luke's head saw what had happened. The girls had tied life jackets to ropes and tossed them to the men. Somehow Sabina had gotten tangled—or was too stubborn to let go—and she had been yanked overboard. Her body had hit the side of the boat before landing in the water.

The boy got a sick feeling in his stomach. He was done trying to lower the dinghy quietly. With the sheath knife, he slashed the rope cables. The dinghy plummeted down through the fog with a splash that might have been a falling refrigerator.

An instant later, he sprinted forward to find Maribel. She was screaming Sabina's name as the men yelled back and forth from the darkness below.

Leon had heard the dinghy hit the water. "What was that noise? Look, look—over there. There's something drifting toward us."

Donny was still scared stiff. "See what? Where'd that little witch go? Boss, she just flew off the boat. You see her? *Flew off like she had a broom* and disappeared."

"Who cares. That's our rubber raft, you ninny! Swim out there and get it. We've got to dump those turtles and crocs before the cops show, and get out of here."

"Dude, she put a hex on me, man! Boss . . . what is a hex?"

"Witches don't wear inflatable vests, you boob. It was a little kid in a Halloween mask. Hold on . . . the raft's drifting closer. I'll get it myself."

Luke realized he'd forgotten to tie the dinghy. Now the tide was carrying it to the men.

He heard loud splashing, and the big man's feet kicking water.

"Got it," Leon yelled. "This freakin' current is strong. I'm not waiting, Menendez. Hump your butt over the side, or I'll leave you here."

Menendez—Donny's last name.

Water thrashed. There were grunts and groans. Through a glowing mist, Luke saw that both men were in the dinghy. Leon was already using one of the plastic oars.

Maribel saw them, too. "Where'd my sister go? You've got to help her!" The girl's voice broke, she was so scared. She had knotted her backpack to one of the big puffy life jackets and was ready to jump over the side.

Leon shot back, "You brats got no business sneaking aboard my boat. That's what the little witch gets for trying to play tug-of-war with an adult."

Was he laughing?

Maribel looked over the railing and saw Luke. "Sabina's not answering!" she cried. "We've got to find her. Grab a couple of those orange life jackets and follow me. We'll tie our packs to them so they'll float. Sort of like rafts."

She dropped through the fog into the water.

The last thing the boy heard before he plunged over the

side was Donny saying to Leon, "Hey, what's this garbage bag doing in our dinghy? And why is it making weird chirping noises?"

Leon growled, "If you don't recognize the sound, you're an idiot. That's why we have to catch those kids before they talk to the cops."

NINETEEN
SWIMMING IN A NIGHTMARE

Sabina wondered if she was dreaming. She remembered throwing a puffy orange life jacket to Leon, that skunk-in-the-weeds. She remembered getting tangled in a rope, and the nasty words the man had used before yanking her over the railing.

The sensation of flying—she remembered this, too. That was all. Now the girl was drifting through a soft silver cloud, which was also a little like flying.

It was a delicious feeling. Eyes closed, she lounged back on a pillow that fit her neck and shoulders perfectly. Her bed was warm, salty to the lips. It floated her along beside a low orange moon that might have been the sun. The sky was brightening.

"Sabina, where are you?" It was her sister's voice.

The girl waved the voice away. "Leave me alone," she answered, yawning. "I'm sleeping."

She heard a splash. Then a heavier splash.

Luke tried to intrude. "Stay away from those guys in the dinghy," he hollered. "I heard them. They plan to kill us!"

This got Sabina's attention. The farm boy wasn't good at inventing stories. The simplest joke had to be explained before he could even fake a smile. So what he'd just said had to be true.

She cracked her eyes into slits. Her head hurt for some reason. When she reached to adjust the pillow, she discovered it wasn't a pillow. It was her inflatable life vest. And her bed wasn't a bed. It was warm flowing water.

The girl opened her eyes wide and tried to blink herself awake. Floating beside her was Carlos the goose. The bird flapped her wings as if she needed help. From the foggy distance came the rumble of men's voices. The wild chirping of what might have been baby birds was louder. The chirping was high-pitched, like tiny sirens.

I've walked in my sleep before, Sabina thought. *But this is the first time I ever swam in my sleep.*

It had to be a dream. The girl was convinced when she

righted herself and saw a giant log cruising toward her. The log was as long as a boat. It had knobby eyes and a sharply pointed snout.

The girl smiled fondly. *A dragon!*

Sabina loved dragons. They had visited her many times in her sleep. Dragons were magical creatures—protective of kids. They could breathe fire and fly. They lived in secret caves.

There was no need to use words when speaking to a ghost. The girl knew this from experience. Maybe the same was true of dragons.

Using her hands, she began to paddle toward the dragon, which still looked like a log. But it couldn't be a log. The thing was only a few yards away, close enough to see details. Logs didn't have white spikes for teeth. Their heads were not jagged with scales.

"Let me crawl on your back," she murmured to the dragon. Her lips moved only slightly. "My head hurts. I want you to fly me home." She beckoned the creature with a welcoming wave.

The creature heard the splash of her hand. It swam faster toward the girl's legs.

The wind stirred. A smoky gray mist swirled down from the sky and blanketed the water. The dragon vanished.

Where had it gone?

The girl squinted. Through the mist, a dark object pierced the cloud. It was tall, curved like the neck of a dinosaur.

The object was familiar. Very familiar. Sabina tried to think back. A pounding headache made it difficult to search her memory. The goose wasn't any help. Carlos hammered the water with her wings like some kind of warning.

The girl's attention shifted. The bird's beak was still taped, she realized.

"You poor nasty goose," she whispered. She reached and stroked the bird's powerful neck. "Don't bite me. I'm tired of you biting me. Hold still!"

Using her fingernails, she ripped the tape free. Carlos responded with a mighty hiss. The bird's chest heaved, breathing in fresh air. After a few croaking attempts to make a sound, the goose used her wings to charge into the fog where the dragon had been.

Sabina heard explosive sounds. The goose's outraged honking. The crash of a huge tail slapping the water.

Her dream was turning into a nightmare. But when she heard a thunderous growl, Sabina's mind cleared.

Finally, she understood.

The dinosaur object in the distance was a dead tree. Luke

had used the tree to anchor their boat while watching Leon and his partner throw a cast net.

And those weren't birds chirping in the distance. They were baby crocodiles calling for help.

The log wasn't a dragon. It was their mother!

Sabina hugged her knees to her chest while the crocodile and the goose battled. Carlos gave a bugling cry. The splash of wings flapping away suggested the goose had escaped—hopefully.

The girl fingered her blue-and-yellow necklace and waited.

Beneath the dark water was a powerful swirl. Something with sharp, rough skin brushed against Sabina's legs. The crocodile spun around and surfaced. Its massive head was only a few inches away from the girl's face. She stared into eyes that were black and catlike. Teeth bristled from the animal's jaws.

There was a chant Sabina had learned from the magic women in Cuba. Her teeth were chattering. It was hard to breathe. It was impossible to remember the exact wording. But she grasped her beads and whispered the magic chant in Spanish.

"I will not fear the terror of night, nor the evil that stalks by day," the chant began. The girl stumbled over several more lines, then concluded, "Danger will not come near me. I am protected. Go away, go away, go away!" She yelled the command three times, as required. "Find your babies and leave me alone!"

The crocodile gave a whuffing grunt. With its pointed snout, the creature nudged the girl.

Sabina couldn't hold it back any longer. She yipped a shrill, chirping scream, "Maribel, I need help!"

The giant croc nudged the girl again after a gentle series of grunts. With a flick of its tail, it swam in the direction of the sinking cabin cruiser.

The high-pitched calls of several baby crocodiles still vibrated through the fog.

TWENTY

LUKE TO THE RESCUE, SABINA DISAPPEARS

Maribel felt trapped when she heard Sabina scream. The men in the dinghy had chased her and Luke into the circle of pilings called Bones Gate. Even a small dinghy couldn't squeeze through the thick poles. For now, at least, they were safe.

Frustrated, Leon stopped paddling. "Why are you kids running from us? We're only trying to help. Climb in. There's plenty of room. Then we'll go find your sister."

There was an oily smile in his voice, threatening.

"For all you know, she could be drowning right now," the man taunted. "Or don't you care? The cops aren't going to like it when I tell them you're the three little thieves who caused my boat to wreck—and wouldn't lift a finger to help that poor little girl."

Luke, desperate to find Sabina, felt his face redden. He and Maribel were clinging to the same piling. They had tied their backpacks there, lashed to a pair of big orange life jackets so they wouldn't drift away. Every time the kids had tried to swim toward Sabina's voice, the men had followed. They had slammed at their legs with paddles and tried to yank them into the dinghy.

"We didn't wreck your boat, mister," the boy hollered. "That's a crock of horse manure."

"Watch your language, kid," Leon snapped, then turned to his partner. "That's how we remember it. Isn't it, Donny? These brats broke into our cabin. The little girl scared you with some dumb witch's mask and you lost control of the wheel. Knocked me overboard. Could've killed us all."

"Yeah," Donny muttered. "Guess so."

The skinny man was still messing with the garbage bag, too scared to look inside. "Boss . . . this weird chirping noise is, like, freaking me out, man. And there's something big slithering around inside there. Why don't we just dump the whole stupid mess overboard?"

Maribel sensed an opening. "Go ahead," she said. "What do we care?"

Donny took that as permission until Leon growled, "Sit down, you nitwit. You still don't get it. There's a hundred thousand dollars' worth of baby crocodiles in that bag. These brats were trying to steal them."

Meekly, the skinny man replied, "Oh. Yeah. But what about that thing in there slithering around? Think it could be—"

"Shut up and pay attention! The moment we look away, those two will make a break for it. It was hard enough to find them in this freakin' fog." Leon thought for a moment. "You got your pocketknife, Donny? Swim over and convince those kids that all we want to do is help. Cut their packs free just in case they're carrying phones."

"Me?" The man's nervous laughter was like ice tinkling. "Boss, I'm not much of a swimmer. And I've never, well, you know . . . I've never hurt a—"

"Do as you're told," Leon ordered. "Those little monsters know too much. Understand?"

The sun was high enough to cast purple light on the nearby mangroves. A dead tree towered above them all. Its trunk was curved like the neck of a dinosaur.

Luke remembered tying up to that tree. Bonefield Key was only a hundred yards away. Close enough for them to wade to shore on this outgoing tide.

He put his mouth close to Maribel's ear. "They'd be stupid to kill us," he whispered. "I think they just want to scare us into not telling the police the truth. But we can't take the chance. We've got to do something fast."

"Like what?" the girl asked. "They'll chase us down. Hit us with paddles again and try to grab us."

Luke came up with a desperate plan. The dinghy was made of rubber. Its flotation tubes were filled with air like an oversized pool toy. Bonefield Key was within easy distance. He and the girls didn't need a boat to go for help.

Their backpacks were tied to a piling and two puffy orange lifejackets. Luke unzipped his pack and took out the heavy camping knife, saying, "Captain Pony said it was an easy walk to her place if the tide was low."

Maribel was close to tears she was so worried. "No! We've got to find Sabina first."

"That's what I mean," Luke said. He was sucking in air and blowing it out to expand his lungs. It was a trick he'd learned while snorkel diving. "I'm going to sneak over there

175

and jab some holes in that rubber boat. When it starts to sink, those jerks won't care what happens to us."

"They'll see you!"

"Not if I swim underwater they won't. If I'm quiet, they won't even know."

"It's too murky," the girl said. "What about all the pilings? Hit one, you could crack your head open."

"I can see better than most," he reminded Maribel.

As they whispered back and forth, Luke laced his belt through the knife sheath. He continued to suck in deep breaths while he pulled on leather gloves. Next, he removed his inflatable vest, then stuffed it into his backpack, which was still secured to the piling.

This was too much for a responsible boat captain. "Absolutely not!" the girl said. "You have to wear your vest."

"I won't be able to dive to the bottom," Luke argued.

Maribel refused. They finally agreed that he could deflate the vest, but he had to keep it on. Later, when needed, he could fill it with air using the manual mouth valve.

"I'll make this fast," Luke said. "If they hear me, take off. Swim with the tide. Find your sister."

"But what about you?"

"Don't worry," he said. "There's something in that

garbage bag those guys don't know about. If they catch me, I'll make sure they find out."

After another big breath, Luke submerged and followed the piling to the bottom. The mud was mushy beneath his boots. The barnacles on the piling were sharp.

He pushed off through the darkness toward the dinghy.

TWENTY-ONE
SABINA, A GOOSE, AND A MYSTERIOUS GIRL

Sabina understood why she still felt dizzy and dreamy when she touched the back of her head. Her hand was covered with blood. Several times she stroked her hair. More blood.

The girl's voice was weaker, too, when she called to warn her sister about the giant crocodile. The croc had been swimming in the direction of the cabin cruiser when it disappeared.

"Get out of the water" was the warning she mumbled. "The croc hears her babies calling. She's coming to find them."

The truth was, the fog was so thick, the girl had lost all sense of direction. Was the sinking cabin cruiser to her right? Or behind her? Even the dinosaur-shaped tree had vanished behind a sparkling curtain that hid the rising sun.

She had to find her way to Captain Pony's house. Maribel and Luke needed help. They required a telephone. But how would she find one?

Sabina made some more feeble attempts to be heard. But her head hurt. She was tired. So she lay back and let her buoyant vest drift her along. Water swirled. Leaves of yellow glided past. The girl couldn't see more than a yard beyond her legs. It was like floating in a silver bubble.

A sudden honking startled her. Carlos skidded through the fog, close enough for Sabina to stroke the bird's powerful neck.

"Sorry I called you stupid," she said. "I'm glad the crocodile didn't eat you—but you've got to stop biting me on the butt."

The goose's orange beak clattered a response. For a while, the bird cruised along beside her, then paddled ahead as if to lead the way.

"Where are you going?" she called.

The goose looked back, then used her webbed feet to paddle faster.

Sabina followed, using her hands and feet to steer.

A low black ledge appeared. It was an island. Mangrove limbs boiled with mist as if on fire. Once again, the goose looked back, then flapped herself through an opening in the trees.

It was shallow here. The girl stood on shaky legs and slogged ashore. There was a path that led to a low mound of shells. She recognized the spot. It was where they had found the graves and wild oranges a week ago.

"Bonefield Key" she whispered, then called to the goose, "You're going the wrong way. There's no telephone here. Take me to Captain Pony's house, you dumb bird."

The goose continued the waddle uphill on the ancient Calusa shell mound.

Sabina stumbled along behind. But not fast enough to keep up. Soon she was lost. Maybe this wasn't the island. Everything—*everything*—looked different. Tree limbs drooped. Water dripped from leaves as if in a heavy rain. Shadows cast an eerie purple light.

Ahead, a massive tree had fallen. Its trunk curved over the ground like a bridge. Beneath the bridge was an opening into spooky darkness. The opening was as black as deep space on a starless night. That vast darkness echoed with the honking of a goose . . . and then what might have been voices.

Sabina felt goose bumps. She stopped. Words on a whispering wind floated from the opening to her ears.

"Stop there," a voice said in Spanish. "It's too dangerous to come closer. I'll find you, sweetie—bless your little heart."

Had Sabina imagined the drawling Southern accent?

Something the girl had not imagined was Captain Pony's warning about Bonefield Key and the Bone Tunnel. *Bad things happen to people who go ashore there,* the old fishing guide had told them. *Some folks never find their way out.*

The opening beneath the tree looked like a tunnel. Maybe it was. How else could Carlos have disappeared so fast?

Sabina's heart was pounding. She took a step closer, then spun around. It was wiser to wait near the shore. Less scary, too.

The girl retraced her steps and sat on a sandy area near the water. The fog couldn't last forever. When the sky cleared, her sense of direction would return. Somehow she would find her way to a road, or a house, and phone for help.

She felt sick with worry about her sister and Luke.

Behind her, a branch cracked. Bushes rustled. Sabina jumped to her feet, ready to run.

"Don't you be afraid, sugar," a voice said. "You're hurt. Your head sure 'nuff is bleeding. That happened to me once a long time ago."

Sabina turned to see a girl about her age. She wore baggy

coveralls with patches on the knees. Red ribbons added color to her long black braids, one over each shoulder. The girl looked small because Carlos was cradled in her arms.

"Who are you?" Sabina said. "Be careful—that goose bites. She hates everyone."

The girl grinned. "Naw, we're old friends. Carlos comes here nosing around a lot—when the moon's right or the sun ain't too bright. This goose is one of the few who knows how to find me."

Sabina touched the back of her head. More blood. She thought, *Am I dreaming? I must be dreaming.*

"Don't matter if you are," the girl replied. "You can see me. Most can't. That's all that matters. Ain't this fog wonderful? It's so . . . private. On mornings such as this, I can go anywhere. Feels like I've got wings."

Carlos fluttered to the ground when the girl offered Sabina an outstretched hand.

"Come on now, little miss. I want to show you something special. You wouldn't have found me if you weren't meant to see it."

Sabina realized she didn't have to speak in Spanish or English to be heard. "See what?"

"The Bone Tunnel, silly." The girl's soft laughter had the

sound of wind chimes. "The entrance is up there where I just came from. But it's too dangerous for someone like you to risk it alone."

Sabina held back. "I want to go to Captain Pony's house first and call for help. Do you have a boat?"

"Don't need a boat," the girl insisted. "Her house ain't far. The water's shallow if you know the way. I've done it hundreds of times. So has Poinciana. I'll lead you there myself later."

"Poinciana Wulfert?" Sabina wondered.

"My sister." The girl nodded, pleased by Sabina's quick thinking. "Our folks moved here from Cuba before we was born."

"Your sister!" Sabina exclaimed. "Captain Pony and I are friends. We've shared secrets. Did you know she's in the hospital?"

"Of course I do. But my sweet sister is soon to be free" was the reply. "Always claimed she wasn't pretty enough to be named after a beautiful flower. That big old tree I just come from? The poincianas that grow nearby have the brightest red blossoms you ever saw—but they ain't bloomed in years. Come on, sweetie," the girl urged. "We don't have much time."

Sabina took the girl's hand. They hiked uphill single file. The wind freshened from out of the moon. An icy light pushed them faster and faster to the top of the mound.

Ahead was the fallen tree. It looked like an amber bridge. Beneath the tree, a curtain of silver fog funneled into darkness.

"That tree's the entrance. Take six steps only," the girl warned. "No more, no less."

Sabina had to hurry to keep up.

"One . . . two . . . three." The girl counted aloud as she advanced, one long, slow stride at a time. "Four . . . five . . . *six*."

The girl stopped. Sabina peered over the girl's shoulder into a tunnel of darkness.

The silver curtain swirled in the breeze. Scarlet blossoms sprinkled down like snow from the branches of a beautiful poinciana tree. Wind gusted. The curtain parted and revealed a large, misty world below.

"Mother of stars!" Sabina exclaimed, stunned by what she saw.

In the distance was a row of pyramid-like mounds. They were built of shells as white as bone. Sparks from cooking fires swirled up from a village of thatched huts. In a valley frosted with fog and moonlight, shadow people danced. Were they members of the ancient Calusa tribe?

That was impossible!

Or was it?

There was something else: An old sailing ship, the kind pirates might have used, was anchored near the mouth of Dinkins Bay. Along the shoreline, men mounted on shadow horses approached. Their swords and silver armor gleamed in the moonlight.

"Who are they?" Sabina wondered.

"Spanish conquistadores!" the girl replied. "The tunnel leads to what happened on this island five hundred years ago. If you took a step further, you'd be trapped there. To me, it don't matter no more."

The strange girl turned in the swirling haze and confided, "My name's Periwinkle. I want to thank you for the prayer you whispered over my grave."

Sabina felt dizzy. Again she touched the back of her head and saw blood on her hand.

Her thoughts shifted to Maribel and Luke. "You've got to take me to Captain Pony's house," she said. "My sister's in trouble. And the boy she's with is the worst you've ever seen when it comes to getting lost."

TWENTY-TWO
REVENGE OF AN ANGRY CROCODILE

Luke pushed off underwater and took three long, slow strokes in darkness, then glided. He searched ahead with his hands and found another piling. The thing was covered with barnacles that tried to slice through his gloves.

He waited for a moment, then pushed off again and took a few more slow strokes.

The key to holding his breath for more than a minute, the boy had learned, was not to rush. Take his time. Use the least amount of energy needed while swimming along the bottom. Trouble was, he had failed to squeeze his life vest completely empty, so he had to battle to stay down.

That seemed like a problem until he banged his shoulder on an unseen piling and shot to the surface.

A big surprise awaited him there.

The dinghy, only few yards away, was barely visible in the fog. The men had found a flashlight and were blinding themselves by shining it around while the baby crocs chirped for help.

"Turn that freakin' thing off, you nitwit!"

Leon's voice.

His partner replied, "Boss—there's something out there. You didn't see it? Take a look. Big, bright-red eyes!"

The light panned along the surface. Luke followed the beam and gulped. The mother crocodile, with her huge head and blazing eyes, was visible in the distance, swimming at high speed.

"You're drunk," Leon growled. "I don't see nothin'. Get in the water. Take your knife and convince those brats to come back here."

"But, boss—"

"Just do it!" the big man shouted. "Or we're both gonna end up in jail."

Luke pulled himself to the bottom and pushed off. This

time he surfaced next to the cabin cruiser. The big boat had sunk as far as it could in the shallow bay. Its engines and rear deck were flooded.

The front of the cruiser angled skyward, held by the piling that had pierced the hull. A single rope hung from the railing. Maribel had looped it there after throwing one of the orange life jackets in an attempt to help the men.

Instead they had used the rope to tie the dinghy to the cruiser so the tide wouldn't carry them away.

Luke unsnapped his knife so it was ready when needed. Silently, he followed the rope to the rubber boat and peeked over the side. Leon sat with his back to him. At his feet was the garbage bag.

A bellowing *WHUFF* vibrated from the distance.

"What the heck was that?" Donny whispered. He switched on the flashlight again. Fog, a curtain of water droplets, became a mirror. The light blinded them both until Leon sat up straight.

"Whoa!" he said. "I saw it—two big red eyes. What is that freakin' thing?"

Fear raised Donny's voice into a trembling soprano. "I don't know, boss, but it's huge. Oh lord . . . and it's coming this way. We've to get out of here!"

Finally, Leon figured it out. The mother crocodile had heard the chirping cries for help. She had chased the men before, but this time they had only paddles, not a fast outboard motor.

"Dump that freakin' bag, quick," he yelled. "Those baby crocs—that's all she wants. Move your butt! I'll untie us."

Luke ducked underwater when Leon spun and lunged for the rope. He waited until the dinghy drifted free to pull his knife. When he surfaced, the big man was swearing at his partner, screaming, "I meant dump them overboard, you idiot! Not in the boat! Now we're really screwed."

Baby crocodiles were skittering around Leon's feet. The rattlesnake was there, too. It seemed confused. Instead of coiling, the snake glided across the deck, over the side, and landed in the water near Luke.

Knife raised, the boy whispered, "It's me. I won't hurt you. Your home's not far from here."

The snake's tongue tasted the air near Luke's arm. The taste must have seemed safe and familiar. The rattler balled itself into a turn, then skated away, doing figure eights across the surface.

"Paddle, boss! Paddle!" Donny begged.

It was Luke's last chance to stab a hole in the rubber boat.

He raised the knife higher, then stopped. *No,* he decided. *This is between them and the crocodile.*

He gave the dinghy a push and swam back to Maribel.

"Did you do it?" she asked. She had to raise her voice because the men were screaming at each other. "I couldn't see much because of the fog."

Before the boy could answer, they heard a lionlike growl and the gnashing of spiked teeth. Water exploded into a series of wild splashes.

"Help me, boss. Throw me a rope or something!" It was Donny's voice.

Luke cupped his hands to his eyes. Leon was hanging on to the sinking dinghy. Donny was close enough to the cruiser that he didn't need additional help.

The giant crocodile had gathered a cluster of babies on her head. With a sweep of her tail, she swam toward the dinosaur-shaped tree and into the fog.

"Let's find Sabina!" Luke gasped, almost out of air. He was untying the orange life jacket and backpack from the piling. "Start yelling her name. Those guys won't bother us again."

They pushed away from the pilings with their life vests inflated. Tidal current, fast as a river, swept them bayward, into the shallows. Maribel took the lead. When her feet touched bottom, she waited for Luke to catch up.

"Sabina!" Several times, she hollered her sister's name.

Luke tilted his head and listened.

"Did you hear that?" he asked. His shirtsleeves dripped water when he pointed to a darkness that was an island. "The goose—Carlos. She's somewhere over there."

Maribel waded ahead through shallow water. The sun was higher now, a yellow disc dimmed by a drizzling haze. She was shivering in her soaking clothes.

For a long time, it seemed, they searched. Another ten minutes passed before Luke stopped and pointed again. "Look—there's Sabina, out there in the middle of the bay. She's either lost or . . . Hey—you don't think she's sleepwalking again?"

It took Maribel several seconds. Because of the fog, her sister appeared to be walking on the water's surface.

"Sabina—wait!" she pleaded, and took off, splashing through the shallows. With her long legs, she left the boy far behind.

Luke was breathing hard when he caught up.

"Her head's bleeding. She needs an ambulance," Maribel sobbed. "Now we're all lost—and I have no idea which way Captain Pony's house is. Do you, Luke?"

Surprised by the question, the boy did a slow turn. "*Me?* Are you kidding?"

Sabina was battling to break free of her sister's embrace. "Let me go!" she demanded. "You might be lost, but Periwinkle's not."

"*Who?*"

"Her," the girl sputtered while she pointed. "That's who I'm following. Periwinkle is Pony's dead sister. She knows where the deep spots are, so you'd better hurry or we'll lose her."

Luke tracked Sabina's gaze to a curl of child-sized gray that seemed to plow a slow path through the fog. But it was the wind. Had to be. There was no person there.

Maribel gave the boy a hopeless look when her sister pulled free and charged away.

"A concussion, maybe?" he asked in a whisper. "She's imagining crazy stuff. What are we gonna do?"

"Catch up and find help," Maribel replied. She was already moving, Luke close behind. "When we see land, I'll run ahead and find a house—or flag down a car or something."

There was no need. By the time they caught up with Sabina, Captain Pony's dock and little boat were visible through the mist.

The goose was on the beach as if waiting for them.

Something else was there, too—a canoe, Maribel thought at first.

No. It was the saltwater crocodile. The croc lay beneath the gnarled old buttonwood tree, mouth open, jagged teeth visible, while her babies chirped from atop her back.

It was Luke who noticed the rubber dinghy—what was left of it anyway. It resembled a deflated beach toy.

"Stop!" he warned. "That jerk Leon and his buddy got here first. We've got to run into the mangroves and hide."

Even Sabina started to follow until they heard a man say, "You gonna let that brat call you a jerk, Leon?"

The three members of Sharks Incorporated stopped and turned. The voice seemed to come from the low limbs of the buttonwood tree—and there they were, Donny and Leon, trapped only a few yards above the crocodile's head.

"You nitwit, just shut up," Leon groaned. Then he said, in a fake tone that was syrupy sweet, "Hey, kids, glad you're okay. We were worried. Really! Is there a way you can help us—without calling the police?"

TWENTY-THREE
POACHERS ARRESTED, CROC EXPERTS ARRIVE

"That was Sabina's mother," Doc Ford told Luke. He was pocketing his phone. "It's good news. Her head needed a few stitches, but there's no concussion. She's gonna be fine— probably home tonight. If not, Maribel will stay with her at the hospital. Hannah will pick them up tomorrow."

They were on the porch of Captain Pony's old house, just the two of them. It had been a wild morning of nonstop activity.

"They'd miss tonight's Halloween party," the boy replied. "And tomorrow's Sabina's birthday." He waited a thoughtful moment. "I'm glad she doesn't have a concussion. Sort of surprised, though, after some of the strange stuff she said.

Do you think the gold medallion Captain Pony told us about is real? And that strange girl? Sabina thinks so."

Doc cleared his throat before speaking. "You're talking about the ghost Sabina claims she saw?"

"Yeah, supposedly," Luke said. "I didn't see anyone. Maribel didn't, either. The girl—or whatever she was—told Sabina that she would find the medallion if she looked in the right place."

"I hope she does," the man replied. "That gold medallion is well documented. It belongs in a museum."

This made sense to Luke.

Doc continued, "The sad thing is, treasure hunters have been digging up Calusa mounds for years looking for gold, which is just stupid. Native settlers had no gold. From what I've read, the medallion was probably made from a Spanish coin. And there were few, if any, pirates on this coast. So there is no buried treasure to find."

"What about her seeing a ghost?" Luke asked. "And a tunnel that could take us back in time? That's not possible, is it?"

The biologist had a nice way of smiling when being careful not to hurt someone's feelings. "A time tunnel? No, afraid not. The same with ghosts, in my opinion. It's a fun idea and all, but . . ." He shook his head and covered his smile with a hand. "Let's just say Sabina has a very active imagination. Creative. In her head, she pictures what others can't see. It's the same with most artists, inventors, people like that. Creativity is a great gift—something I wish I had."

"Me too," Luke agreed. "I'd love to see a ghost. Or go back in time five hundred years."

"Wouldn't that be great?" the man replied. "Get a first-hand look at how the Calusa people lived. Things have changed since then. The sea level would have been a lot lower. And there'd be animals that haven't been seen in Florida for a hundred years or more—monk seals. Ivory-billed wood-peckers. And more great white sharks, because seals were so common here."

Doc went through a list of extinct or endangered species before adding, "That's historical fact, not fantasy. See, Luke, there's so much to learn about the real world—this bay, the oceans—I don't waste my time on fairy tales."

"Makes sense," the boy said. "But Sabina claims the time tunnel *is* real. I can usually tell when she's lying, and she wasn't. She had to have seen something that convinced her. I wonder what it was."

"She didn't tell you?"

"Not the details. She started to but got mad when I laughed. That Sabina's got a temper. Thing is . . . there are times I really do believe her. A lot of the weird stuff she says turns out to be true."

"Understandable," the biologist said. "You're teammates. Trust is important. Sometimes there's not much difference between what's real and what's not—if a person believes." He got up from his cane-backed chair. "Did you hear a truck drive in? That could be my friend the crocodile expert."

Yes, it had been a wild, action-packed morning they had just experienced. There had been police cars, a police boat, and an ambulance, all with flashing lights. Next there were a lot of questions from officers in uniforms. Sabina had been bundled onto a stretcher—despite her protests—while Doc had distracted the crocodile long enough for police to arrest Leon and his partner, Donny.

Seeing the police cuff those two creeps and lead them away had been the most exciting part of the day—so far. Kind of scary, too. Leon, before ducking into the squad car, had given Luke and Maribel a nasty, burning look.

"I think he's threatening us again," Maribel had told Detective J.D. Miller when it happened. The detective was another friend of Doc's. He was a nice man who had learned to trust the kids when they'd helped bust a band of shark poachers that summer.

"Put those two losers out of your mind," the detective had replied. "Our water-patrol guys found about fifty rare turtles on that fancy boat they claim you wrecked. Mostly diamond-back terrapins. And we expect to find more evidence when we search Leon's house."

A year ago, Leon had been found guilty of selling more than four thousand rare reptiles on the black market, the kids learned. A half-million dollars' worth. Poaching had made Leon rich.

With a smile, the detective had added, "But this time the judge will put those guys away for a good long stretch. The turtles, plus Maribel's video of them netting baby crocs, will be more than enough. Crooks like them are going to learn not to mess with the members of Sharks Incorporated."

Luke still felt good about that. He'd been up most of the night but didn't feel tired. No way. It was nice hanging out with the biologist. And there was more excitement to come.

"Yep," Doc said, going down the porch steps. A white pickup truck had pulled into the yard. "That's my friend

Doctor Frank Mazzotti. A great guy—you'll like him. Hmm. Looks like Frank brought only one helper. But if it's the person I think it is, that's more than enough. They're two of the country's most respected experts on American crocodiles."

Looking over his shoulder, the biologist added, "It's a good thing you stuck around, Luke. Get some gloves on. Are you ready to catch and tag that saltwater croc?"

TWENTY-FOUR
LUKE HELPS TAG A CROCODILE

The noon sun had burned the fog away. The crocodile lay on the sand near the buttonwood tree. Several baby crocs jetted into the water when they heard the scientists approaching. But the mother didn't budge. As a warning, she slapped her head against the sand, hissed, and opened her jaws wide.

Dr. Frank used his hand to signal: *Stop.* He was a large man in loose pants and a baggy blue shirt. He wore red-tinted prescription glasses. Tufts of gray hair curled out from beneath his floppy hat.

"Stay back for a sec," he said. "Laura and I will tell you when we need help—if we need help. We've done this a lot. No one gets hurt. That's the important thing. For us and the crocodile."

Laura was Dr. Laura Brandt, a regional scientist for the US Fish and Wildlife Service. Dr. Laura was slim and athletic, and also dressed to avoid the sun. Over one shoulder she carried a bag that contained electrical tape and a bunch of other stuff. Dr. Frank carried a long pole with a wire noose on a swivel taped to the end.

Luke realized that Maribel and Sabina would feel left out if he didn't get video of what happened next. He sprinted to the porch and returned with the waterproof camera.

Dr. Frank was explaining the situation. "Let the croc calm down for a minute. We don't want to spook her into the water. If she does go in—and she might—that will require a whole different capture-and-tag technique. We'd need to use a walk-through snare, maybe. Or floating nets. It's a lot more complicated."

As the man continued speaking, Luke raised the camera and touched Record.

"Crocs aren't as aggressive as alligators," the expert explained. "A gator, if you use a head noose, will practically tear your arm off—even with a breakaway noose like this one. A gator will roll and keeping rolling. Most crocs, though, only roll a couple of times before they settle down. Ask Laura. She's dealt with a lot of ornery alligators."

Dr. Laura replied by speaking to Doc Ford. "I'll circle closer to the croc's head. Once Frank gets the noose on her, I'll cover her eyes with a towel and tape the jaws closed. That's where you come in. We might need some help getting her tied. But stay away from her tail." She looked at Luke as she said this.

"Could break your leg or crack a rib," Dr. Frank warned. "If we do everything right, the croc will be free and on her way in no time at all. No lasting stress, perfectly healthy. She's probably lived sixty years or more in the wild, and we sure don't want to hurt her now."

Luke watched the experts go to work through the camera lens. It was so exciting he was tempted to stop recording and use both eyes. But he kept the camera steady. The crocodile fought back at first, then lay still after her jaws were taped shut and her legs were tied.

Working smoothly, the scientist took all sorts of measurements. Dr. Laura dictated the details into her phone while Dr. Frank shot photographs. They hunched over the animal with what might have been a medical kit. Luke couldn't be certain and didn't want to interrupt.

"She's a big one," the man announced. "Three-point-four meters—more than eleven feet long. And heavy. Well over five hundred pounds, wouldn't you say, Laura?"

Dr. Laura was doing calculations on her phone. "Closer to three hundred kilos," she replied.

"The metric system," Doc Ford translated for the boy's benefit. "That's almost seven hundred pounds. About ready to mark and tag her, Frank?"

His friend took this as a signal. He summoned Luke, saying, "Do you have gloves on? Good. Put down that camera for a few minutes and give us a hand."

The men straddled the crocodile while Dr. Laura steered Luke closer to the animal's back. They knelt. She unrolled a bag of tools and pointed. "See the two rows of scales along the croc's tail? They're called scutes.'"

"Scutes?" the boy repeated to fix the word in his head. To him, the jagged scales resembled rows of teeth on a buzz saw.

"The scutes are pretty much the same on every croc in Florida," the scientist explained. "If we remove a couple, though, the missing scutes will make the animal easier to identify. Not just any scutes. We keep records—like a sort of code."

Dr. Laura continued, "On this crocodile, we're going to remove the third scute from the left row of her tail. It won't hurt her a bit. Hand me that knife."

Luke did as he was told.

The jagged-looking scute came off as cleanly as a finger-nail clipping. It was deposited into a small container.

Next, the scientist removed the second scute from the right side of the croc's tail. It went into the same container.

"All done," Dr. Laura said after she had cleaned the areas. "This big female is now officially American Crocodile Right-Scute-Two, Left-Scute-Three. Every croc we catch is marked differently. Right-Scute-Five, Left-Scute-Four. Right-Scute-One, Left-Scute-Six. Like that. All based on which scutes we remove. See how it works?"

"Not really," Luke admitted. He was on his feet, backing away.

"It's not as complicated as it seems," the scientist said in a kindly tone. "Later, if she's recaptured, or even seen, we'll note which scutes are missing. That will tell us she's American Crocodile Right-Scute-Two, Left-Scute-Three. We can chart her movements and track her growth. These are rare animals. Very important to the ecosystem. We'll monitor her and her hatchlings and try to make sure they stay healthy and safe."

"Stand back, everyone," Dr. Frank said. "I'm going to cut her loose. We'll give her all the time she needs to recover. When you're a safe distance away, just stand quietly and watch. It shouldn't take long."

It didn't. Luke shot video of the crocodile high-walking into the water. With a thrust of her huge tail, she submerged and rocketed away like a torpedo.

"You did a great job," Dr. Laura said to the boy. "Doc told us that you and your friends are the ones who found the croc. Was it somewhere near here?"

"Just a few hundred yards away," he replied, motioning. "It's a little island with shell mounds. Think she's on her way there now?"

"Could be," Dr. Frank said. He was typing information into a laptop. "When you saw her, did you smell sort of a musky odor?"

"Yeah, I did. Not strong, but musky," Luke said.

The scientist nodded. "That's probably where her nest was. You've got a good sense of smell. Doc also told us that you and your friends are experts at handling a small boat. That you tag sharks for him."

"We're still learning," the boy replied. "But we do okay, I think. My teammates, Maribel and Sabina—I wish they could have seen this."

"Maybe they will, when we come back," Dr. Frank said. "That island you mentioned—I don't suppose you'd be willing to stop there occasionally and check on how the croc's doing? You know, take pictures and video. But keep your distance, of course. It's best if the croc doesn't know you're there. Doc has my e-mail address."

Sabina would have taken this as an opportunity. Luke did, too, but it was harder for him to say, "Yeah. Uh, sure. If you want. In fact, my friends and I were hoping to camp there over Thanksgiving vacation."

The crocodile experts both looked at Doc Ford. "That's not up to us but, sure, great," Dr. Laura said. "Can you talk to their parents, Doc? A week of daily monitoring would be very helpful. Oh—there's one more thing. Frank, do you want to tell him?"

Dr. Frank smiled, pleased by the suggestion. "When a young person helps Laura and me tag a croc, we let them pick out a name. Any name they want. It goes into our data bank, and the croc will have the name for the rest of its life. Interested, Luke?"

"You're saying I can give that crocodile a name?" The boy frowned, unsure. It wasn't like a seven-hundred-pound croc was a dog and would come when called. And it didn't seem right to do something so important unless his teammates were involved.

This gave him an idea. What if he combined the sisters' names?

"How about"—Luke had to picture the spelling in his head—"how about Sabina-Belle? Would that be okay?"

"Sabina-Belle," Dr. Laura said, making notes on her phone. "Beautiful. Love it. Sabina-Belle it is. From now on, that's her name."

Doc Ford gave the boy a private look of approval. "Wise choice," he said.

TWENTY-FIVE
RETURN TO BONEFIELD KEY

Thanksgiving vacation began on a Saturday, the day before what astronomers called a supermoon. It had been four weeks since the police had arrested Leon and his partner.

Finally, it was safe to return to Bonefield Key.

Or so they believed.

Doc Ford explained, "A supermoon only happens when the moon is at its closest point while orbiting the Earth. 'At perigee' is the term they use."

Luke repeated the word in his head. *Pear-ah-jee.* He pictured a pear hanging close to the marina to anchor the word's meaning.

"Thanks for letting us borrow your telescope," the boy said. "We'll take good care of it."

"If we didn't trust you kids, you wouldn't be here," Doc replied. "Have fun—explore around with the scope. A dark spot in the sky doesn't mean there's nothing out there to find."

Luke scratched at the jagged scar on his shoulder. He liked the image that produced on the secret screen inside his head.

"Stars and planets, sure," he replied. "Probably lots of them up there somewhere."

That morning, Doc, Captain Hannah, and their infant son, Izaak, had followed the trio to Bonefield Key in Hannah's fast skiff. The kids had already unloaded supplies from their much slower rental boat. After a busy hour helping the kids set up tents, a firepit, and the hammock and going over safety rules, Doc and Hannah were getting ready to leave.

They stood at the water's edge. Izaak slobbered and cooed while his parents offered last-minute advice.

"Even without the telescope, the moon will look a heck of a lot bigger than usual," the biologist continued. "You three picked a good week to camp. But this time"—his voice became stern—"stay out of trouble. Keep that handheld radio with you at all times."

He turned to Sabina. "Is that clear, young lady? The police might have more questions. And all they want to hear is—"

The girl's face reddened. She glared up at the man. "I know, I know," she interrupted. "No more stories about being rescued by a ghost. I'm not crazy, and I'm not a liar. So I must've imagined everything. Fine! I've got five stitches in the back of my head to prove it."

Actually, the girl's stitches had been removed two weeks ago. To cover a strip of shaved hair, she wore a red bandanna tied at the back like a pirate. The bandanna was a birthday present from Captain Pony.

The old fishing guide was still in the hospital after suffering another stroke. Doctors weren't sure if it had anything to do with the fall she'd taken. The kids had visited her often. With Hannah's help, they had continued to look after the property and feed her animals.

Maribel felt a tad guilty about the situation. If Pony had been healthy, able to take care of the place, they probably wouldn't have been allowed to spend five nights camping here, only a few hundred yards from the woman's house. They could have fed the animals and monitored the crocodile easily enough with daily trips from the marina.

"We'll be just fine," Maribel said after giving Captain

Hannah a hug goodbye. "I'll check in every two hours and leave the radio on when we go to bed. Plus, we have this now."

She held up another present from Pony Wulfert. It was the ancient shell horn made by the Calusa people long, long ago.

A person had to be at least eighteen before applying for a Coast Guard guide's license, but Maribel proved that she'd been studying. "Five short blasts on a horn," she said. "That's the danger signal for boaters. We won't need it—but just in case."

"We probably wouldn't hear it anyway," Doc said. "So use the radio. And make sure to check on that crocodile at least once a day—but from a safe distance. My crocodile-expert pals want to stop back and tag those hatchlings."

He stepped aboard the skiff. Hannah followed. She started the engine and began a slow turn. "If you find more oranges," she hollered over her shoulder, "gather all you can. And take lots of pictures." She took one hand off the wheel long enough to emphasize something else. "Remember—try to find a small citrus tree healthy enough to give to the experts. A seedling or a sapling that would be easy to transplant."

The woman had provided the kids with a folding camp

shovel just in case. The state of Florida was still looking for a way to combat the terrible citrus greening disease. Survivor trees and their seeds were desperately needed.

It was a good feeling to finally be on their own. Luke volunteered to cook dinner and wash the dishes even before they had decided on what to eat.

Sabina loved the idea. Maribel disagreed. "Not fair," she said. "The cook shouldn't have to clean up. We take turns."

On 4-H campouts Luke had noticed that the kids in charge of cooking often left a terrible mess, unconcerned because their part of the work was done. Cooks were a lot tidier if they had to do both jobs. To him, this made sense.

"We can still take turns," he added. "Either way. It's up to you. And don't forget, you owe me. I named the crocodile after you and your sister."

Sabina had to fight back a smile. It wasn't easy to chide the farm boy after he'd done something so sweet. "Whatever," she said. "I think you're just trying to get out of building our tree house."

Luke's jaw tightened. He'd spent hours cutting poles and lashing them together with rope. True, he had goofed up by building the platform on the ground. The thing was so darn heavy, he'd had to take it apart, then haul it pole by pole into the limbs of a nearby gumbo-limbo tree.

A table made of bamboo stalks lashed to a stump had been a bigger success. And a heck of a lot easier to make.

"Looks pretty solid to me," Luke argued, without looking up.

Sabina did. She stared at the tree. To her, the tree house looked as if a flood had left a mess of rope and logs trapped in the low limbs.

"Maybe so," she said, "but you'd better build the roof fast. I don't want to sleep in a bunch of bird poo."

He thought that was unlikely until he noticed the osprey. It was perched on the platform, watching them.

The boy tried to spook the bird by waving his arms. *Are you trying make me look nerdier than I am?* he thought.

Pee-pee-peep-peep, the osprey chattered, as if taunting. It didn't budge.

"There's something you haven't told us," Sabina said. "That bird knows you. Follows you around like a dog. Come on, farm boy. The morning you and Maribel got lost in the fog, I remember that osprey landing on Captain Pony's porch. Almost like it was keeping an eye on you."

Luke didn't respond.

It was Maribel's turn to be offended. *You got lost, not us!* she wanted to say. She backed off, though, when her sister's eyes moved to the old gravestones. The graves were not far from where they'd set up camp.

"If it hadn't been for your pet osprey," Sabina continued, "Periwinkle might have stuck around and let you see her instead of disappearing. Like most ghosts, she's shy around normal people." Glaring at Luke, she warned, "Don't you dare laugh at me again!"

Periwinkle—the imaginary girl—was a sensitive subject. Sabina's head injury had not been serious. No concussion, just a bad bruise and a cut. But the doctor had warned their mother that the girl might be moody until she fully recovered.

Moody? Sabina was *always* moody—especially when it came to spirits, poetry, and ghosts.

Maribel slapped her hands together as if washing the subject away.

"It'll be dark in two hours," she said. "We still have a lot to do before dinner. We need more firewood, and those beans have to soak. The corn, too. I want to get an early start in the morning and find that orange tree."

They had brought cooking gear. It included a cast-iron skillet, a heavy Dutch oven with a lid, plus tin cups and plates—not plastic. The kids had retrieved so much plastic trash from the bay that they avoided the junk whenever possible.

The Dutch oven had been Captain Pony's idea. She had written down a few recipes from her hospital bed. Some included strange, old-timey ingredients the kids had never heard of. There was "fatback," "lard," "red-eye sop," and "swamp cabbage."

Other ingredients were more familiar. And they'd brought a big cooler filled with ice and all sorts of good things to eat.

"I don't know what swamp cabbage is," Luke said. "I'm hungry enough, it sounds sort of good. But there's a deep spot under the mangroves that's loaded with oysters. I might be able to find a few clams while I'm at it."

Sabina's mood brightened. She was hungry, too. "Maribel and I will catch some fish—but you have to clean them. We catch, you clean—that rule stays the same."

Luke and Maribel had both learned that, outdoors, the easiest way to get along was to do more work than was expected, and never complain.

"I'll have the cleaning table ready," the boy replied, and wandered off toward the water.

When he returned, his pants were wet up to the knees. He had waded the edge of the bay and cut two mangrove roots covered with oysters. The old fishing guide called them "raccoon oysters" because raccoons loved eating the things at low tide.

Pony's recipe was simple: Toss the mangrove roots on the fire. When the oysters were fully cooked, the shells would open on their own.

While the girls fished, Luke went back to work on the tree house. Thick tubes of bamboo became a ten-foot ladder to what he was trying to build. The bark of the gumbo-limbo tree was reddish amber. It had muscular limbs that grew away from the trunk at different angles. Because of this, the platform he'd made was an uneven jumble, not flat.

The boy puzzled over the problem while the osprey observed from above. The bird chattered and whistled as if offering advice.

"Quiet, I'm thinking," he replied, then looked up through

an umbrella of green leaves. Some of the higher limbs, he noticed, looked strong and straight.

A new idea came into his head. The platform didn't have to be tied to the lower limbs. It could hang from the tree like a giant swing. The trunk and the crooked limbs might serve as anchors.

Luke got busy. When the girls returned an hour later, they were impressed.

"What do you think?" he asked.

What had been a jumble of poles was now a solid deck ten feet above the ground. There was plenty of room for sleeping. A roof of palm fronds was already under construction.

Grinning, the boy sat with his legs dangling over.

"I told you he could do it," Sabina bragged to Maribel, which wasn't true. "Get down here, farm boy. We caught some nice ones. You have fish to clean."

TWENTY-SIX
CAPTAIN PONY AND SABINA SHARE SECRETS

At sunset, dinner was ready: corn on the cob and baked potatoes, skins black, hot from the coals. There were slabs of fried sea trout served with a sauce of butter, sea salt, and juice from fresh key limes. Black bean soup was ladled out over rice.

The Dutch oven was still wedged against the fire.

That was worth waiting for. Inside, wild guava, pineapple, and papaya slices had been topped with honey and cinnamon, then covered with a pie crust. Captain Pony Wulfert's recipe again—except for the pie crust.

Luke had cheated. He had used a biscuit mix from Bailey's General Store.

"Hold it. We forgot something," Sabina said before

anyone could touch their food. They were seated around the bamboo table. Smoke from the fire helped keep the bugs away. White birds, necks curled, crossed an orange sky in a slow V formation.

Luke snapped his fingers. "Hot sauce for the oysters. Yeah. You're right."

"Not that," the girl said. "This."

From beneath the table, she raised the ancient shell horn. "It's a sunset tradition, Pony told us. Good luck before a meal."

The girl curled her fingers deep inside the shell. She blew hard and blasted out three squeaky notes.

To keep from laughing, Luke had to look at the ground.

"That did not sound like a fart!" Sabina glared. "Don't be gross."

Maribel was laughing, too. Then they were all laughing until, suddenly, one by one, they went silent.

From the darkening shell mound came a distant reply— the faint, strong note of what might have been a horn. Then two more notes echoed as if signaling from a cave.

Stunned, the kids looked at one another.

"The Bone Tunnel." Sabina whispered this too softly for the others to hear. *Good.* The old fishing guide had warned that people would not believe until they saw it for themselves. She had also told Sabina how to avoid the dangers of entering the tunnel on a full moon.

"Try the horn again," Luke urged.

Maribel grabbed the shell from her sister's hands. "Don't. It could be someone at the marina. Doc and Hannah might think we're in trouble."

Sabina was staring at the nearby gravestones. A ray of sunlight painted the rough pioneer concrete with gold.

She got to her feet. "It's Periwinkle. She's calling for me. I've got to go."

"Wait—please," Maribel begged in Spanish. "Let me try the horn. I'm sure it must be someone at the marina. You know how sound travels over water."

She started to translate for Luke until he interrupted. "I understood. Some of it, anyway. Go ahead. Blow it again."

Maribel was good at just about everything. Sabina was used to this irritating fact. She took a seat and glowered while her sister produced three clear bell tones from the ancient shell horn.

Silence. Flames in the fire pit crackled. The osprey, eyes alert, ruffled its feathers and scanned the trees. Somewhere, roosting owls exchanged baritone calls.

Hoo-hoo looks for you? the owls seemed to ask. *Hoo-hoo's looking for you?*

"Barred owls," Luke said softly. "Doc took me out and showed me one night. Said they're kinda rare on Sanibel. Rat poison and stuff might have killed most of the owls because they eat rats. Owls, yeah. That's what we must've heard."

"You know it wasn't an owl," Sabina snapped. She was about to say something else but was stopped by a series of distant hoots and honks.

Maribel sighed with relief. She smiled. "That's Carlos! It was just the goose calling, not a horn. Isn't it funny how our imaginations go wild in a place like this?"

Sabina had to bite her lip to stay silent.

There was a reason. The girl hadn't told Luke and Maribel everything about that foggy morning. She'd told them about Periwinkle, yes. And she would have described seeing Spaniards on horseback and a Calusa village if Luke hadn't laughed.

But that wasn't the only reason: Sabina wasn't sure if it had really happened. She'd been so dizzy after hitting her head. Now, only a few weeks later, it all seemed like a dream. Had she imagined it?

The only person she had told was Captain Poinciana

Wulfert. They had talked often in the hospital—always in Spanish—just the two of them alone.

The old fishing guide had believed every word of Sabina's story. The woman had shared a few secrets of her own—including the exact spot where King Carlos had spoken to his dead ancestors. She, too, believed there was a mysterious tunnel there that led back in time.

"They'll all think we're both bat-daft loco," Poinciana Wulfert had whispered from her hospital bed. "It's best we keep this to ourselves."

Now, sitting by the fire, Sabina was aware that Luke was studying her reaction. On his face was the same irritating look of doubt. The girl took a deep breath. She forced a smile. "I'm starting to like that goose," she said sweetly. "I'll give Carlos some extra corn in the morning."

Luke sensed the lie. It added a gray-brown glow to the girl's face. The lightning eye behind his forehead was seldom wrong.

"Yeah, it definitely wasn't a horn we heard," he said to put the subject to rest. "It was that crazy goose. Let's eat."

He got up and returned with a bottle of hot sauce for the roasted oysters.

An invisible moon rose a half hour before sunset. By seven

it was midway up the eastern sky. The moon wouldn't be full until tomorrow, yet it was bright enough to cast shadows while Luke finished the dishes.

Sabina had retreated to her tent to work on a new poem—she claimed.

In fact, the girl had snuck away to reinspect the grave markers made of pioneer concrete.

The poachers had used a shovel to dig around the smallest marker. A layer of shells, as big as rocks, had protected Periwinkle's grave—and a secret that Captain Pony had told only Sabina.

The old fishing guide had been dazed after coming out of surgery. She had gotten the names of her thieving neighbors wrong when speaking privately with the girl.

In Pony's confused mind, their names had become Ponce Leon and Don Pedro.

Leon and Donny, Sabina thought bitterly. *Those skunks-in-the-weeds.*

Weeks before they were arrested, the men had broken into Pony's house. They'd stolen an old journal.

"They're after the gold medallion," the woman had confided, taking Sabina's hand. "Truth is, I don't know where it is. Periwinkle took it into the Bone Tunnel the night she died, and the medallion disappeared. You have to find it, Sabina. You've gotta! Or my dear sister will never be at peace."

"And do what with it?" the girl had asked.

"You'll know when the time comes" was the reply. With a dreamy smile the woman had added, "When I leave this world, I'm giving Bonefield Key to the archaeologists. I'm trusting you, my little *nieta*, to do what is right."

This had brought tears to Sabina's eyes. Captain Pony had never had children. In Spanish, *nieta* meant "granddaughter."

TWENTY-SEVEN
LOST SOULS

Sunday morning, church bells sailed across the bay. The chimes mixed with the mangrove silence of wind, birds, and a crackling campfire.

Home seemed a distant world away from their tidy little camp on Bonefield Key.

The kids had already boated to Captain Pony's house, where they'd fed and watered the animals and done other small chores. They were starving when they returned. Their breakfast consisted of hot cocoa, oatmeal, broiled fish, and badly burned toast.

Sabina had managed to drop four slices of bread into the fire.

Luke scraped off the black edges, slathered a piece with

sea-grape jelly, and folded it into a sandwich. "Pretty good," he said, munching. "In fact, I like this toast better. Crunchier. You know? Sort of like burned bacon. The wood ashes give it a nice salty taste."

Sabina took this as a compliment. "Instead of being a poet, maybe I'll become a famous chef."

This made good sense to the boy. "I'd rather eat than read, so yeah. A chef probably makes more money. But I'm not sure dropping food in a campfire counts as cooking."

"It's called being creative," Sabina argued. "Poets can't waste their time making money. We have to write about love and sadness and being poor—too poor to buy a computer-game console that would look really nice in my bedroom."

It was Maribel's turn to do the dishes. "Mama wouldn't let you have that even if we could afford it," she chimed in, pouring water into a shiny tin basin.

"I have plenty of other sad things to write about," Sabina countered. "In Havana, near our house, was the most beautiful cemetery in the world. Huge, a whole city of marble tombs where dead people live."

"*Live*?" Luke asked.

"Forever," the girl responded. "No smart person would leave a cemetery as nice as that. My favorite poet is buried there. I used to take flowers to her grave and eat a sandwich. That made me sad, too. I loved the place. If I ever get rich enough, I'll buy a spot next to her."

She looked over her sister's shoulder. The basin containing the water was shiny enough to show Maribel's reflection.

This reminded Sabina of a favorite poem: "The Mirror" by Dulce María Loynáz. It was also a chance to share something important that Captain Pony had told her in the hospital.

"Would you like to hear the poem?" the girl asked. "The writer's first name is Dulce María. Dulce means 'sweet' in English. She was a beautiful young Cuban girl like me. I used to read verses at her grave."

Sabina cleared her throat. In a low, theatrical voice, she recited the first few lines:

> The mirror hanging on the wall,
> where I sometimes see myself in passing . . .
> is a dead pond brought
> into the house.

The boy gulped the last of his cocoa, suddenly in a hurry. "A poem about a dead pond in a house—yeah, that sure sounds fun. But I've got to get back to work on our tree house."

"Wait and just listen for a minute," Sabina insisted. "That book by the archaeologist that Pony knew? At the hospital, when she woke up from her surgery, she told me something interesting."

It was sort of interesting, Luke had to admit. At first, anyway.

The Calusa believed that all people had three souls. One soul lived inside a person's eyes. A second soul lived in the mirror image of a person's face when staring into a pool of water.

Sabina motioned to the shiny tin basin. "I remembered when I saw Maribel's reflection."

"What about the third soul?" her sister wanted to know.

This part was more complicated, Sabina said. The Calusa people believed that a person's shadow was more than just a shadow. When the moon was high and bright, the shadow came alive.

"Came alive?" Luke didn't want to hear any more. The old fishing guide had suffered a stroke, so it was just another imaginary story. More nonsense.

Stroke. The word sounded so simple—unless a kid knew

what the heck it meant. Luke did. Three years ago, before his mother died, a nice doctor had told him, "A stroke is sort of like a heart attack. But it happens in the brain."

Something to do with a blood clot or reduced blood flow, the doctor had explained.

"Nothing to worry about," the doctor had assured him. "Most people recover and do just fine. If we're lucky, your mother will be the same great lady she was before this happened."

Luke's mother had not been one of the lucky ones.

The memory of those final weeks was painful. Something—the drugs or the brain surgery—had changed her. It was like his mother lived in a fantasy world.

The same was probably true of Captain Pony.

There were no such things as time tunnels and ghosts. As Doc had said, *There's so much to learn about the real world—this bay, the oceans—I don't waste my time on fairy tales.*

Doc's opinion was good enough for Luke. But he didn't want to hurt Sabina's feelings by saying the old lady's stories were silly. Maribel, however, deserved the truth—even though the subject was so upsetting he was already near tears. Over his shoulder, he gave the older sister a concerned look before he walked away.

They had fished together so often, she understood.

"I'll be there in a second," she whispered. "But first I've got to radio Hannah or Doc and tell them we're okay."

Check in every two hours. Maribel was good about following rules.

TWENTY-EIGHT
LUKE MAKES A DISCOVERY

Luke climbed to a high limb above the tree house he was building. He adjusted one of the many ropes rigged to keep the platform flat. They were strong enough to support the weight of several adults, plus the bamboo walls and roof that would come later.

Maribel had yet to appear. It had been twenty minutes since she'd whispered, *Be there in a second.*

This was unusual for a girl who was never late.

Radio problems, the boy decided. Maybe she and Sabina had taken the rental boat to the old lady's house to use the phone. Better yet, the canoe Pony had loaned them. In the shoals off Bonefield Key, a canoe was just as fast.

That was okay. From where Luke sat, twenty feet above

the ground, there was a lot to see. A wedge of Captain Pony's tin roof was visible. To the west was the salt pond. The giant croc, Sabina-Belle, lay on the bank basking in the sun, her babies nearby. She seemed to be doing just fine despite missing two scutes.

To the east, a pyramid of trees marked the highest point of Bonefield Key's shell mound. Sprinkled among the leaves were specks of color, round like balls.

Luke touched the burn scar on his shoulder. He shaded his eyes and zoomed in. Yes . . . they were oranges, as bright as Christmas ornaments.

The boy wiped his red eyes and sniffed. Great! Now he knew where to look.

He was straddling a limb, head bowed, when Maribel called his name from below. "I talked to Hannah," she hollered. "You're not going to like it. We've got to go back to the marina in the morning."

"Huh?"

She said it again, adding, "We can leave our tents and stuff for now. But tomorrow night—maybe the next few nights—we can't stay here."

"What are you talking about? I could have the tree house finished by tomorrow afternoon."

Maribel realized the boy had been crying when he climbed down and rearranged a pile of bamboo to avoid looking at her.

"You're upset. Did something happen?"

"Nah, stupid ants," Luke lied. "I poked myself in the eye slapping at some. There must be a nest up there. Why did Hannah say we have to leave?"

Out of kindness, Maribel didn't press the issue.

"Because they're letting Leon out of jail in the morning. He still has to appear in court—I didn't get all the details. The police want us to stay away from Captain Pony's property for a few days."

Luke still didn't understand. "Those guys won't mess with us. They're already in enough trouble. The cops found all sorts of illegal animals locked up in that building next to Leon's house."

"It's more complicated," the girl said. "Doc and his friend the detective want to keep an eye on Leon. They think he might try to rob Pony's house again. Those weren't Hannah's exact words, but I figured it out. So this is our last night camping here for a while."

Maribel thought for a moment.

"Dr. Marion Ford."

She said this in a musing tone that was familiar to Luke. No matter where they went, the quiet, kindly biologist often worked with police or tough-looking military types. Later, he refused to discuss the reasons.

"I'll never understand him," the girl added. "He wouldn't hurt a fly. Can you imagine Doc getting into a fight? Or pulling a gun on some bad guy? He'd have to take off his glasses and clean them first."

Normally, this would have gotten a laugh from Luke. He had tried to picture it before—Doc scribbling in his notebook despite the blazing gunfire of a SWAT team. Or Doc in an old Hollywood Western, fumbling for a six-shooter, then diving into a water trough so he could watch what happened next. Soaking wet, the notebook, of course, would come out again. Every small detail had to be recorded.

The biologist wasn't a coward. No way. The kids knew this. He was just a . . . well, a nerdy scientist who cared more about collecting data than saving his own life.

But Luke didn't laugh. Not even a smile. Leon was a big, tough, loudmouthed bully. Doc was no match for a drunken thief who, the boy now believed, would've killed him and the Estéban sisters rather than go to jail.

Maribel's voice interrupted his thoughts. "Luke? *Luke.* Are you okay? You wanted to talk about something. What's wrong?"

He needed a moment to edit what he had planned to say.

"It's about the old lady. The stuff she told Sabina in the hospital. After a stroke, sick people don't think straight. They can say some really strange things."

Maribel agreed. "The story about shadow people coming to life. And the Bone Tunnel. I understand."

"I'm not so sure you do," Luke said. He returned to stacking bamboo. "Before my mother . . . Well, you know about that. During her last weeks, it was like she lived in a dream world. She told me things that I knew weren't true. That could never be true."

"About you?"

The boy nodded.

"Like what?"

No way was Luke going to share his mother's last words of advice—or the predictions she had made about his future.

One day you will be a very famous man, his mother had promised while in a feverish daze. Several times she had insisted it was true.

Another silly fairy tale. No way that would ever happen.

"I'm talking about the old lady," Luke insisted. "She's not in her right mind. That stuff about ghosts and some secret tunnel where time has stopped. It's all"—the boy had to clear his throat to hold back tears—"it's the sort of happy crap that sick people say before they die. If Sabina believes it, fine. I just thought you ought to know the truth before we make fools of ourselves tonight."

He loaded his arms with bamboo and started toward the tree.

Maribel walked after him. "You're not going to tell me what your mother said. Are you?"

Without looking back, the boy shook his head.

There were times when Maribel wanted to take Luke into her arms and hug him like the brother she'd never had. But she couldn't. Since being struck by lightning, the boy had built an invisible wall around himself. Or maybe he had always been that way.

The best she could do was give his shoulder a gentle touch. "I don't believe Captain Pony's stories, either. Not about a time tunnel, anyway. But I don't see any harm in following Sabina when the moon comes up. Let her find out the truth for herself. This will be our last night on the island for at least a few days."

Luke sniffed. He cleared his throat. "Fair enough," he said. "Come on. I want to show you something."

They went up the bamboo ladder. Maribel commented on how solid the platform felt beneath her feet.

"Are you sure you those are oranges?" she asked when Luke pointed to the pyramid of trees. All she saw was a jungle of leaves.

"It's the only part of the island we haven't explored," the boy replied. "Where's your sister?"

"Down here," Sabina hollered. She stood at the base of the tree, dressed in boots and gloves, still wearing the red pirate bandanna. In her hand was the machete they'd been allowed to bring. The tool had been useful during a day spent gathering food. "It's time to start supper. I think we should explore some more tonight."

Maribel followed Luke down the ladder before sharing Hannah's upsetting news. She expected Sabina to be angry. Instead the girl became oddly silent. She stood there squeezing her beaded necklace as if listening to an unheard voice.

Sabina was—a wind-chime voice that gave her goose bumps.

"Something bad is going to happen," she said finally. "I think Leon's already out of jail. He . . . he might be on his way to Sanibel right now. Or already here!"

"What makes you think that?" Maribel asked.

Luke was shaking his head. He was tired of fairy tales. "The moon will be up soon," he said. "We still have time to find that orange tree. I vote we eat later."

TWENTY-NINE
THE SURVIVOR TREE

In a modern world of parks, bike paths, and golf-course communities, the hike to the top of the mound would've taken twenty minutes.

But this was Florida the way it had been for centuries. It was hot, the temperature in the eighties even this late in the day. Heat radiated up from a century of seashells piled into what might have been a pyramid. But it was now jungle, trees forty feet high. Every weed, bush, limb, and vine battled for space and a glimpse of sunlight to survive. Overhead, the foliage was so dense, it was rare to see a patch of sunset sky.

Maribel and Luke took turns with the machete. They hacked a path uphill through a wall of green. Sabina lagged behind. In her head, the wind-chime voice continued to warn, *You're in danger. Something bad could happen tonight . . .*

The older sister sensed Sabina's problem. She waited until Luke was ahead of them to say, "I get feelings like that all the time. You know, that I'm in danger. Or about to have some bad luck. Everyone does. And I'm almost always wrong."

"I'm not everyone," Sabina replied. "And I'm almost always right." She spun around as if she'd heard a twig snap. "Did you hear that?"

"No. What?"

Luke didn't notice, he was so busy chopping a path.

"What if he's here already?" Sabina whispered. "What if he's following us?"

"You mean Leon?" Maribel gave her sister a reassuring look. "He doesn't get out of jail until tomorrow. Besides, I have this." She unclipped the handheld radio and held it up to illustrate. "Do you want me to call Hannah just to be sure?"

"That's smart. Do it now," Sabina said. She continued to search the darkening trees behind them.

Maribel squeezed the radio's transmit button. "Break-break, calling Sanibel Biological Supply," she said into the radio. "Do you copy?"

The name of Doc Ford's business was Sanibel Biological Supply. On the porch of his house was a VHF marine radio that scanned for calls.

Static was the only reply.

Maribel cleared her throat. "I'll try a different channel," she said.

The girl tried several channels. Same thing. No one answered. Just static.

Maribel battled a slow rush of fear. "The trees are too thick for the signal to get out," she said calmly. "Relax, it's no big deal. Doc or Hannah will hear me when we get to the top of the mound."

Sabina muttered, "That skunk-in-the-weeds bully. Leon would love to catch us out here all alone." She tilted her head skyward. "Where's Luke's stupid osprey when we need that mean bird?"

In the silence that followed, a mother raccoon and two furry babies went scampering through the brush behind them.

Relieved, Maribel laughed. "That's what you heard. See? We're not in any danger."

Sabina didn't believe it. But when the osprey appeared overhead and circled, she took this as a good omen.

"Besides," the girl reasoned, "Periwinkle will help us if

we're in trouble. This is where she stays day and night—unless there's a heavy fog."

The imaginary ghost again.

By sunset the kids had battled their way to the top of the ancient mound. They were soaked with sweat and tired. Finally, they saw oranges dangling from high limbs in the distance.

But from which tree?

It was impossible to tell. Trees of all sizes grew here in a jumble.

"Let's spread out," Maribel suggested. "Start shaking limbs. If an orange falls, you'll know you've found the right tree."

To the left, below the mound, Sabina saw a splotch of water. It reflected a wafer of copper light that was the rising moon.

"I know where we are," she said. "The morning you two got lost in the fog? There was a path that led me to a great big tree. It was as wide as a bridge. That's the opening to the . . . to the . . ."

The girl almost said *Bone Tunnel*, but caught herself. She didn't want to be laughed at again.

People won't believe you anyway, Captain Pony had warned. *They'll think we're both bat-daft loco—unless they see the tunnel for themselves.*

They will, Sabina decided.

The timing was perfect. A huge moon would soon cast shadows and provide plenty of light to explore.

The old fishing guide had also told her, *Find the gold medallion. You'll know what to do when the time comes. The spirit of my poor little sister will finally be free.*

I will, Sabina vowed again silently.

"Sure, spread out," she said to Maribel in a normal voice. "That's smart—explore on our own. If I find that path, it'll be a lot easier for us to get back to our camp."

Luke was all for splitting up. *Drink more water than you think you need* was a team rule. He had. Now what he really needed was a private place to pee—the sooner the better.

"Take the machete. I've got my knife," he said to Maribel, and hurried off.

When he was comfortable again, he puzzled over the oranges hanging overhead. There were dozens. But they weren't clustered in one spot. They were scattered in a strand over a broad area.

Weird, he thought. *That's not the way fruit grows in most orchards.*

The boy zigzagged through the foliage, shaking limb after limb. No oranges fell. He came to a clearing. This made no sense either until he saw the remains of a gigantic tree lying flat on the ground.

It took him a moment to figure it out. Long ago, when the giant had fallen, the trunk had smashed every living thing around. Now only saplings grew in the area. They were skinny trees and very, very tall. Oranges appeared to dangle from the scrawny limbs.

Interesting. Hannah had said the citrus experts wanted young survivor trees to transplant. Maybe he had made an important discovery.

Luke approached the fallen giant. The trunk was waist high and six feet wide. He threw his arms over the thing and climbed up. The tree became a bridge that allowed him to walk among the skinny saplings. They were covered with thorns. Huge thorns, sharp, three inches long. They were dangerous looking, just as Hannah had described.

She was right about wearing gloves, he thought, and gave one of the skinny trees a shake.

Thump-thump-thump. Several oranges landed on the ground nearby.

Same with the next tall, skinny tree. And the next.

The trunk of the fallen giant arched over a mound of old seashells six feet below. His head tilted up, then downward. That was when the boy realized the saplings weren't trees. Not really. They were new limbs growing from the underside of the fallen tree he was standing on.

Was that possible?

He got down on his belly and confirmed it.

Amazing. This old giant of bark and moss was a living citrus tree. The thing had to have survived hundreds of years before it fell. Yet the giant had refused to die. Its new limbs were still producing big, healthy fruit.

"Over here!" he yelled to the girls. "I found it, I found it! The survivor tree!"

The osprey had been following Luke until then. Suddenly, though, the bird soared off like a fighter jet, screaming, *SAR-SAR-SAR!*

The wild cries sounded like a warning.

Luke was too excited about what he'd found to suspect that Leon might be following them.

THIRTY
CAPTAIN PONY'S SECRET PLACE

One look at the giant tree, and Sabina knew what Luke had discovered. It was a spot known only to the old fishing guide and her sister, Periwinkle, who had died after falling from the same tree more than sixty years ago.

This was another secret that Captain Pony had shared in the hospital.

Maribel and Luke were busy shaking limbs and trying to catch oranges before the oranges fell into a basin of shells below. They didn't notice that it was getting dark until the moon appeared.

"There it is," Maribel said. "Look behind us, Luke."

To the east, the moon was the size of a frozen sun. It floated weightless and huge in blazing silence. Black craters etched eyes and a crooked smile, all encircled by smoky blue rings.

"Ice crystals way up in the sky," Luke remarked. "That's what Doc said." He kept his voice low. "We should get back to camp and use the telescope. Where's Sabina?"

Sabina had been waiting for this moment. "I found the path," she called. "Follow me. I want to prove I'm not crazy."

The opening to the Bone Tunnel awaited.

Just like on that foggy morning weeks ago, the narrow path turned and twisted downhill toward the bay. Maribel and Luke followed. Each carried a sack of oranges.

"Look at our shadows," Sabina said over her shoulder. "When's it's darker, our shadows will be the size of giants. That's the way Pony described it. Now do you believe I've been here before?"

This was true. Sort of. The moon cast light at a low angle. The milky beams connected Luke's feet to a human shadow that was taller than he was. But not gigantic.

"Shadow people. *Right*," the boy responded. "You can tell us all about it when we get back to camp. I'm hungry."

"Not until you see the opening for yourselves," Sabina shot back.

Luke was running out of patience. "The opening to what?"

"You'll find out" was the reply.

They continued downhill to where they had a view of the ancient tree. The trunk curved like a bridge over the basin of shells. Sabina stopped and looked beneath the tree. Moonlight created what appeared to be a misty curtain. A pile of oranges, newly fallen, had collected there after rolling downhill.

"There it is. The opening to the Bone Tunnel." Sabina sounded confident. "Come closer and look for yourselves. But you have to do exactly as I say. It's dangerous."

Maribel placed her bag on the ground. Concerned by her sister's behavior, she spoke in Spanish. "Dangerous? How? Are you still worried about Leon following us?"

Luke understood some of what she'd said. Not much. To the left was the bay. Water glistened with moonlight and the last silver rays of the setting sun. They'd been dopes to hack their way to the top of the mound. Camp was only a few minutes away if they had waded along the shoreline. It would have saved them a lot of work.

The boy studied the area beneath the fallen tree. "I don't

see any tunnel," he said in English. "But I do see a bunch of oranges, and I still have some room in my bag. I'll grab a few, then we'll head back to camp."

He started toward the basin of shells.

"Don't!" Sabina shouted when he got to the tree. "Stop right there. Not another step! That's where Periwinkle died on the night she tried to return the gold medallion."

Startled, the boy turned. The look on his face asked, *Are you nuts?*

"If you take more than six steps," Sabina insisted, "you could be trapped in . . . trapped in . . ." The girl paused, suddenly unsure of herself. Had she had really seen Spaniards on horseback and a Calusa village? Or had it all been part of a dream?

"All I know is, something bad is going to happen," she finished in a stubborn voice. "I warned you, so don't blame me."

With a shrug, Luke ducked beneath the fallen giant and walked toward the pile of oranges. Seven . . . eight . . . nine . . . ten steps—Sabina counted each long stride in her head.

Nothing happened. No misty curtain parted. There were no sparks from Calusa cooking fires. No Spaniards with gleaming swords.

Maybe I was dreaming, the girl finally had to admit. She watched as the boy continued several more yards, then knelt over another new discovery.

"Hey! Come look at what I found!" he hollered.

At Luke's feet, in a ribbon of moonlight, grew a tiny orange tree, only two feet tall. The trunk and limbs were spiked with thorns. Maribel joined him. To be sure, she removed a leaf from the tree, crushed it, and held it to her nose. The tangy citrus odor was unmistakable. "Perfect," she said. "A pretty little sapling orange tree. This is exactly what the scientists need."

"It's too small to be called a sapling," Luke corrected. "Sprouts this size are called seedlings. But it sure looks strong and healthy. Wish we hadn't forgot the camp shovel."

"Let me try," Maribel said. She squatted beside him and used the machete to trench around the little tree. After several minutes of digging, she muttered, "The tree's roots are all tangled in a great big seashell. Sabina, do you have a flashlight? We need it."

The girl approached reluctantly at first. Her worries vanished when she recognized the seashell that her sister was trying to pry free. It was a horse conch—almost exactly like Captain Pony's ancient Calusa horn.

The roots of the little tree had woven themselves through three holes in the shell. The holes had been precisely drilled. A longer root protruded from the center of the crown. The shell's pointed end—the apex—had been sawed flat like the mouthpiece of a trumpet.

"That's just like the horn we left back at camp," Sabina said. "It must have belonged to Periwinkle. I was right. She was *here*!"

Maribel and Luke were too busy digging to listen. Gently, gently, after several more minutes, the seedling tree finally came free in Maribel's hands. The huge old shell horn provided a solid base for the roots. The way the tree sprouted from the shell, healthy and green, it might have been a trophy from a garden show—or a 4-H project.

Maribel's voice was shaking, she was so excited. "Shine the flashlight," she said. "There's a lot of dirt inside this shell. But I hear something else clinking around in there."

"Oh my stars," Sabina whispered when she saw what spilled into her sister's hand.

It was the gold medallion.

Now it was Maribel who felt as if she were dreaming. The medallion was smaller than imagined—half the size of her palm. But it had weight and warmth. The strange designs they'd seen in the old drawing were there, but very faint.

Two square holes for eyes stared back at the kids from what might have been the head of an alligator—or a crocodile. Beneath the eyes were fangs. Or teardrops.

Luke noted circles within a circle above the eyes. He was studying the moon when the sound of a fast outboard motor caught his attention.

"A boat's coming," he said in a rush. "Give me the flashlight. I'll flag them down."

"No!" Sabina protested. "It might be Leon. I told you something bad was going to happen. I can feel it."

Luke didn't have witchlike powers, but he did have excellent hearing. "It's not Leon, or his creepy partner. I recognize the boat. I've heard that engine lots of times."

The boy was right. He grabbed the light and ran to the water's edge. Soon Doc and Hannah appeared in Hannah's fancy skiff.

But Sabina was right, too.

Earlier in the day, something terrible had happened.

THIRTY-ONE
SURVIVORS

It was Hannah who gave them the first piece of bad news. The police had released Leon that morning, not tomorrow as planned. The man was free, so they would have to leave Bonefield Key right away.

When they returned to camp to pack, the trio got another shock. Something—or someone—had gone through all their stuff. Their tent was a mess. The jungle hammock had been turned inside out.

Maribel felt goose bumps when her sister announced, "Pony's shell horn is gone. I was right! Leon was here looking for us. Can you imagine what he would've done if he'd found us all alone?"

Luke wasn't worried until he saw the concern on Doc's

face. "Leave your gear and go with Hannah," the biologist ordered. "Do it *now*. She'll take you back to the marina. I'll come later in the rental boat after I've had a look around."

On foot, the man circled out into the dusky moonlight alone.

The members of Sharks Incorporated did as they were told.

Hannah waited until Doc was at the marina, tying up the rental boat, to give them more bad news. They were gathered near the marina office when she finally said, "There's no easy way to put this. The hospital called. Pony Wulfert died this afternoon. She left a letter addressed to you kids. And a separate letter for you, Sabina. The letters are in the lab if you want to read them. Doc will be up there in a minute or two. Or would you rather wait until your mother gets off work?"

Sabina ran toward the lab, yelling, "No, that can't be. I should have been with her!"

Luke and Maribel followed in a daze. They hadn't had time to tell Hannah much about the ancient survivor tree they'd discovered. And it didn't seem right to show off the gold medallion without Doc present.

The biologist didn't stick around long enough to allow that to happen. There was so much shock and confusion, only Luke noticed when the man slipped away and sped off toward Captain Pony's house in his larger, faster boat.

Maybe he was upset by the sound of kids crying.

Hours later, the boy changed his mind. The moon floated huge over the water when he saw the strobe of blue flashing lights at the mouth of Dinkins Bay. Was the mysterious biologist working with the police again?

Probably.

It made sense. Someone had torn their camp apart. The police were investigating. That was proof enough for the boy.

The next morning, in the lab, Doc told the kids what had happened during the night. He was at his desk icing a swollen left hand—the result of a fall, he claimed.

Luke's suspicions were right. Detective Miller had found Leon inside the old lady's house, trapped in a closet by a furious goose. Scratches and tufts of missing hair suggested that Leon had also been attacked by another type of bird.

"An osprey or a hawk of some type," the biologist guessed. "If so, that's not as unusual as people might think. Animals can be very territorial. They have incredible instincts when it comes to targeting anything—or anyone—who poses a threat. How they know is still unclear to science."

Perplexed, yet amused, Doc added, "Like that big mother crocodile. The police were surprised to find her lying in the yard like she was waiting for Leon to come out. A coincidence? Could be. But I doubt it. Instinct is a form of intelligence. It's born into just about every living thing—animals and plants. That croc wouldn't have survived for sixty years if she had ignored threats like Leon."

Picturing the big croc, Sabina-Belle, Luke grinned. Even Sabina managed a smile. They sat at a metal table, tired but alert after a long, restless night. Positioned between them was the little seedling orange tree. It was rooted solidly in the ancient shell horn. Nearby, atop two envelopes, lay the gold medallion.

The envelopes contained the letters that Poinciana Wulfert had written only a few hours before her death. The handwriting was shaky and ornate. It was the sort of penmanship taught at small, old-time country schools.

The kids had been unable to read most of it. Now they were waiting for Hannah to return. The woman had made copies of the letters and taken them to a friend of hers, an old circuit-court judge, for advice.

Doc's head tilted as if he'd heard a gate close. He stood, his hand still wrapped in a towel. "Here she comes now, with Izaak. I'll take care of the baby while you and Hannah talk privately."

On his way out, the biologist turned. His expression was serious, but his eyes were warm. "Pony Wulfert was a true Florida pioneer. She would have died alone and lonely if you kids hadn't come along. You made her happy. She *trusted* you. Thing is, trust between friends can be complicated. It's a gift. But trust is also an obligation. Think about that when Hannah tells you what those letters mean."

"Congratulations," he added from the doorway.

The screen door banged shut.

Maribel glanced at Luke. *Congratulations?* For what?

Sabina remained silent. Fondling her cowrie-shell necklace, she stared into space. She didn't need a letter to understand Pony's last wishes. The same was true of Pony's dead sister, Periwinkle—now that they'd found the gold medallion.

256

Hannah entered the lab carrying an official-looking box that had been sealed with tape. Instead of her usual fishing shorts, she wore dark slacks and a starched gray blouse.

"The judge is an old family friend," she said, "but I wanted to dress in a way that showed respect for Captain Wulfert. Pony was one of the finest fishing guides in this state. It wasn't easy back then for women. I'm not the only one who owes her a debt for the courage she showed."

Hannah had placed the box on Doc's desk. She noticed the gold medallion and the envelopes beneath it. "Those are the last two letters Pony would ever write in her life. They prove she loved Florida and its history as much ... as much"— the woman's voice caught—"as much as she cared about you three kids. Especially you, Sabina."

The girl sniffed and managed to say, "I know. I'm almost always everyone's favorite. But I couldn't make out her writing. What do the letters say?"

Hannah stroked the girl's hair. She spun a chair around and sat facing the trio. Instead of opening the envelopes, she used the copy she'd shown her friend, the judge.

"'I, Poinciana Wulfert,'" Hannah began in a clear, formal voice, "'being of sound mind and memory, and not crazy no matter what folks think, declare this to be my last will and testament. When I pass into the next world, I want everything done exactly as I say. So pay attention!'"

Hannah couldn't help smiling at that. She read a few more lines, then gave up and folded the paper. "Might be easier," she said, "if I just explain. Pony's attorney was with her at the hospital and let her put most of it in her own words. There are other documents not included in those envelopes—all signed and witnessed with her attorney present. That's important, legally speaking. The judge agreed."

Luke's attention had drifted to the window. The osprey was dive-bombing Pete, the curly-haired retriever. The dog seemed to be enjoying the game.

"I still don't understand," Maribel said. "What does an attorney have to do with the letters she wrote to us?"

Hannah waited until Luke was listening. "Because Pony left all her property to you three kids. She had no family. No friends, either, at the end. Just her animals—and you. It's not official yet, but there shouldn't be any problem."

Luke cleared his throat and said, "Property? What are you talking about?"

Maribel felt numb. Tears began to flow. "Do you mean she left her house—everything—to us?"

"Bonefield Key, too," Sabina whispered.

"Temporarily," Hannah said. "In a trust—that's a legal term. State archaeologists and citrus experts will be involved. The property, the shell mounds, and the survivor tree will always be protected. It's what she wanted. Captain Pony was a smart, tough lady. Taking care of her property will be a big responsibility. But she knew that you three could handle it."

There was more. Hannah opened the official-looking box. It contained items that police had recovered after arresting Leon. She removed several old books and some aged photographs in frames. Finally, she took out Pony's ancient shell horn. It was similar to the shell horn on the table.

"These all belong to you, Sabina. Oh, and there is something else." Hannah had to battle a teary-eyed smile. "Her goose. Pony wanted you to have her goose. That was in the letter, too."

Sabina sat straighter. "That mean goose? I inherited *Carlos*?" She grimmaced, but then her face softened.

Find the gold medallion and you'll know what to do, the old fishing guide had said in the hospital. *The spirit of my poor little sister will finally be free.*

The girl stared at the shell horn where the little survivor

tree grew. Her eyes moved to the strange gold ornament once worn by a Calusa king named Carlos.

Suddenly, she understood. The medallion belonged in a museum. It was the only way to protect the ancient shell mounds from treasure hunters.

"Captain Pony was a survivor, too," Sabina said softly.

In her head, the old fishing guide's last words whispered like wind chimes.

The spirit of my poor little sister will finally be free.

Author's Note

Before thanking those who contributed their expertise, time, and patience during the writing of *Crocs*, I want to make clear that all errors, exaggerations, or misstatements of fact are entirely the fault of the author. This applies, in particular, to those good people who provided information about American crocodiles, archaeology, archaic Spanish citrus, life in Florida a hundred years ago, and Native American sensibilities.

A key source was Dr. Frank Mazzotti, one of our nation's foremost authorities on crocodilians. Years ago, I had the pleasure of accompanying Dr. Mazzotti and my pal, author and naturalist Peter Matthiessen, on a wild night hunt for crocs in Florida Bay. If I had any previous doubts that the field sciences could be exciting, they vanished that moonless eve in Little Madeira Hammock. With Frank at the tiller, using headlamps (when needed), we boated through the mangrove labyrinth in search of sparking red eyes that signaled the presence of *Crocodylus acutus*. We waylaid and "tagged" several smaller crocs using the same technique as described in this book.

Southwest Florida's indigenous people, the Calusa, also play a key role. I have tried to portray their history and the shell mounds they built (a few of which still exist) accurately, but keep in mind that much is based on my personal interaction with mounds the Calusa people once inhabited. Experts such as Dr. William Marquardt and Dr. Karen Walker have done their best to keep me on the straight track, and I say again: errors or inaccuracies, if any, are entirely my fault.

Of special concern to these fine archaeologists is an ancient gold medallion that you have read about within. The Calusa people had no gold—save for a few coins, perhaps, salvaged from Spanish shipwrecks. My own research confirms there were no pirates on this coast, so there is no buried treasure to find. Yet even now, the mounds are occasionally damaged by uninformed lawbreakers who go at them with picks and shovels.

The medallion, however, is real. I know because I rescued it from the shyster who stole it. Years later, I donated this rare artifact to the Florida Museum of Natural History in the name of the child who found it. (For more on this tragic story, read my Doc Ford novel *Ten Thousand Islands*, or my nonfiction book *Batfishing in the Rainforest*.)

The "strange designs" carved into the medallion are accurately described. Interpretations of their meaning, however, are mine alone. To a lesser degree, the same is true of the medallion's relationship to King Carlos (or King Caalus) who ruled Southwest Florida at the time of Spanish contact. It is not known if the medallion was buried with Carlos, or if he had been beheaded, but the story has been part of local lore for decades.

Finally, I would like to thank Tina Osceola, associate judge of the Seminole Tribe of Florida; Captain Esperanza Woodring; and Steve Smith, executive vice president of Gulf Citrus Growers Association, for adding or vetting other details as shared in *Crocs*, the third offering in my Sharks Incorporated series.

—Randy Wayne White
Casa de Wendy
Sanibel Island, Florida